NO
PLACE
TO
HIDE

NO PLACE TO HIDE

Dan Latus

ROBERT HALE

First published in 2018 by Robert Hale, an imprint
of The Crowood Press Ltd, Ramsbury, Marlborough
Wiltshire SN8 2HR

www. crowood.com

British Library Cataloguing-in-Publication Data
A catalogue record for this book is available from the
British Library.

ISBN 978 0 7198 2618 4

Typeset by Jean Cussons Typesetting, Diss, Norfolk

Printed and bound in India by Replika Press Ltd

Chapter 1

He hardly ever thought of the past. Why would he? It held few attractions for him. Plenty of outstanding questions and problems, but none of them interesting or urgent enough to overcome the certain knowledge that the past – his past – was too uncomfortable a place, dangerous even, to visit.

In the evenings, after supper, he liked to sit on the covered terrace outside the villa, a glass of the local red wine to hand, and listen to the woman singing softly to herself as she cleared up in the kitchen and made things ready for the next day. She was good at homemaking. He appreciated that, and he was getting used to it.

The woman was called Magda. So she had told him, at least. They had been together since shortly after he arrived here, but he had never known how long she would stay. He still didn't. She hadn't said, and he hadn't asked. He preferred to leave it that way. For that matter, he had no idea how long he himself would stay. As she seemed to do, he took it one day at a time.

This wasn't where he had planned to spend the rest of his life, but it wasn't a bad little place. The villa was comfortable, and it had everything he needed in a house. The small town nearby was OK, too. Boring as hell, perhaps, but he'd come to appreciate boring. It was another word for safe. He didn't mind a town that was boring.

The woman, Magda, seemed to feel the same way. He didn't kid himself about her, though. He didn't have any illusions. She wasn't here because of him, any more than he was here because of her. They had both simply fetched up on this distant shore, two of a kind, with a common need. Then they had somehow found and hung on to each other, and stayed together. Until now. That was all it was.

They probably weren't the only ones in that position, either. São Brás de Alportel, deep inland in the Algarve, was a town where all sorts of people ended up, a least-bad-option kind of town. Nothing wrong with that. Nothing at all. It was far better than the resorts along the coast, where ex-pat criminals and the flotsam and jetsam of life gathered, along with the holidaymakers and the golfers, and where trouble broke out as regularly as the tide came in. Not here, though. There was a lot to be said for the inland, wooded hills of the Algarve.

But now he suspected his time here was coming to an end. He knew that, could feel it in some intangible way he didn't understand but could still accept. He sensed that soon he would be leaving, and probably not by choice.

The woman finished in the kitchen. She came out onto the terrace to stand behind the chair where he sat. She wrapped her arms around him. He pressed his cheek against her forearm for a moment, and pressed his lips against the warm softness of her skin. Then he sat up and reached for the bottle to pour her a glass of wine, and himself another one.

'So warm,' she murmured, blowing a gentle stream of air across his face.

He nodded. 'And very humid, surprisingly.'

She thanked him for the wine and sat down next to him, glass in hand. Then she turned her head to gaze out across the little garden, and the almond trees and the ancient olive grove beyond.

'I like these evenings so much,' she said.

'Me, too.' He smiled, studied her face for a moment and added, 'Something on your mind?'

'I do love being here with you,' she said with a sigh.

'But?'

'But it will not last much longer, I think.'

'No?'

She shook her head. 'My grandmother was Roma – gypsy. She could sense these things. And so can I.'

'Superstition,' he said with a smile, but wondering all the same how she knew.

'Perhaps.'

She shrugged and took a sip of her wine.

'You worry too much,' he said gently. 'You're such a pessimist.'

'Perhaps,' she said again. 'We will see.'

What did she know, he wondered. How odd that her forebodings coincided with his own. Perhaps it was an infection? But, in that case, which of them had developed it first?

'An early night?' she asked with a smile, as she finished her wine.

'That's a good idea.' He smiled back at her and held up his own glass. 'You go. I'll come just as soon as I finish this.'

'Don't be long,' she said, slipping away.

He listened, without hearing her, as she made her way through the house. She was such a quiet person, he reflected. And not only in the house. She seemed to move through life the same way, too, making no sound and leaving no trace. It was how she was. Almost a talent. He never heard her.

He heard everything else, though. The house creaked and groaned as it cooled and settled for the night. The tops of the palm trees around the house rustled in a breeze he could neither see nor feel. The cicadas were busy tonight, too.

He sat up, yawned and rubbed his face. The air was heavy and tiring. In the distance, but not so very far away, thunder rumbled. No doubt another dry storm in the offing. There wouldn't be rain, not here, not yet. Closer to the town a dog barked. Others, troubled by the approaching storm, and on high alert, responded.

Then the phone rang, its old-fashioned shrill tone startling him as it reverberated through the house. He willed it to stop, but it took no notice. So in the end he had no choice. It had to be answered. With a grimace, his heart beating fast, he got to his feet.

Chapter 2

Once the guard was securely bound and gagged, he gave him a vicious crack on the head with a home-made cosh. Then he opened the door, pushed the unconscious guard inside and climbed into the back of the van himself, slamming the door shut after him. After a quick change into staff uniform, he moved up front, alongside the driver.

'Move it!'

'Will he be all right?'

'Never mind him. You've been told what to do. Now do it!'

The driver thought about arguing for a moment. Then he changed his mind. With a grimace, he started the engine and put the van in gear. They moved off. With the clearance he had, doors and gates opened automatically.

Five minutes later, the van stopped briefly in a supermarket car park, next to an open-sided shed with a clear plastic roof, where the trolleys were parked. The man got out. The van took off.

As soon as the van was out of sight, the man stepped forward. A black BMW turned a corner and approached quietly. It came to a gentle stop. The man opened a rear door, got in beside the passenger and slammed the door shut.

'All right?' the passenger asked.

The man nodded. 'I soon will be. Let's go.'

Five minutes later Edward James Fogarty began to relax. He even smiled. He was on his way. What could be better than this? Well, getting his life back and settling a few scores. That would be better. But this was a good start.

Everything had gone smoothly so far. Just as it should do if you planned things properly. He could kiss the lot of them back there goodbye now, however many uniforms they had looking for him.

And they would be looking, he thought with a grim smile. There was no doubt about that. News of his escape would be big enough to cause a few heads to roll, which was something to look forward to and savour. For today, though, this was good enough for him. He was out.

Chapter 3

The number on the caller display wasn't one Jake recognized but the code made him pause and grimace again before pressing the button. A call from the UK was unlikely to be good news.

'Boa noite?' Good evening.

A pause. Then, 'That you, Jake?'

He smiled with relief. It was a familiar voice, a gravelly Geordie voice, and one he was glad to hear.

'How are you doing, Bob?'

'Never better, bonnie lad! Can't complain at all.'

'That makes one of us, then.'

The other man laughed. Then he paused a moment before saying, 'Bad news, I'm afraid, Jake.' After another pause, he added, 'He's out. You know who I mean. We need to talk. We need to meet.'

Jake grimaced. He knew what that meant.

'You still there, son?'

He roused himself and ran his tongue experimentally around the inside of his mouth. 'I'm still here,' he said, struggling to stay calm and keep his voice even. 'When was this?'

'A couple of days ago. During the exercise hour.'

That figured. Open air – and opportunity.

'Where was he?'

'Belmarsh. The high security unit.'

He nodded. That's where he would have guessed, if he'd

ever allowed himself to think about it.

'They didn't manage to keep him very long,' he said, not bothering to hide the bitterness he felt.

'No, they didn't. You're right, son.'

Bob speaking in a quiet, soothing tone now. Trying to placate him, wanting him to stay reasonable. Not pour obscenities down the line, and hurl the phone away in anger and disgust.

Just a few months, Jake thought. Hardly any time at all. He shook his head. They should have done better than that.

'So what happened?'

He heard Bob sigh. Could almost see him shrug with frustration.

'I'm not really sure. There's talk of a helicopter being involved, but I don't know the details.'

Helicopter? But of course! It would have to be on a grand scale, wouldn't it? That was the man all over. Think big, act big – be big! He shook his head, more angry and frustrated than ever.

'Tell you what, Jake. I'll come over to see you in a day or two. I'll have found out a bit more by then.'

Jake was ambivalent about that, much as he liked Bob. It would involve risk. Even the best operatives could be followed, or tracked, one way or another.

'Let's leave it for now,' he suggested. 'There's not that much of a hurry, is there?'

'Whatever you say, Jake. But there's something else I need to tell you. I'm pretty sure he knows where you are.'

That was another shock.

'Not exactly, perhaps, but the general area.'

'That's not good,' Jake said as evenly as he could manage.

'No, you're right. It isn't.'

'How's that happened?'

'Who knows? A tip-off, maybe. He'll certainly have had people looking. You're not the only one in the frame, either. There's Nicci, for one. Remember old Nicci? You used to get on well with him, didn't you?'

'Well enough, I suppose. But we were hardly best mates.'

'Point taken. Anyway, he's a target. And the others, of course. There must have been a leak somewhere. My information is that Fogarty has found out where you all are. Your own situation being a bit different doesn't really help much. You're as much at risk as the rest of them. So we'd better talk about it. OK? Meet me in Faro.'

They didn't say much more. It was an open phone, and they were both well schooled in the precautions needed.

'Look after yourself, son.'

'And you, Bob.'

The other man chuckled. 'Oh, you don't have to worry about me, bonnie lad!'

No, perhaps not, Jake thought as he put the phone down. Bob would be all right.

He wouldn't be, though. Nor would Nicci, or the others. They were all at risk, just as Bob had said. But he couldn't say it was a total surprise. More like inevitable. He had felt something coming for a while. This must be it.

Chapter 4

Magda had come back out on to the terrace, dressed in a sheer nightdress that clung to her like the finest silk. She looked at him questioningly. He shrugged.

'Is it time?' she asked.

'Time?'

But he knew what she meant. They had both been expecting something. Now this. Time? It looked like it was.

She reached for the wine bottle and poured them each another glass. He nodded his thanks. She smoothed her hand across his cheek and sat down across the table from him.

'Is it bad?' she asked.

'Bad enough,' he admitted with a sigh.

He was grateful she didn't press him for details. Instead, they sat in silence for a couple of minutes, while he sipped his wine and considered his options, and she just waited.

Frankly, he thought, his options were rubbish, absolute crap. None of them offered the safety he had thought – until now – that he had here. He grimaced. If not yet a disaster, the situation was galloping towards being one.

Fuck it! He wished, not for the first time, he had never got involved in the first place. It would have been better, far safer anyway, to have stuck with being bored, skint, and having nothing to do.

Too late for thinking like that, though. Far too late. Fogarty was out, and would be coming for him. And for the others. Bob was right.

'We could go to my country,' Magda suggested.

'Your country?' he repeated with an ironic chuckle. 'How would that help?'

'I don't know.' She shrugged. 'But it is far from here.'

'Hm.'

She got up to go back inside.

Her country? He smiled ruefully. He didn't even know for sure what, or where, that was. Poland? Russia? A territory that used to be part of the Soviet Union? Somewhere like that, he had always supposed. Eastern Europe, anyway, or even beyond.

He didn't fancy that very much. They had long winters there. All those countries. Hard winters, as well. Worse even than winters in his own country, to which he wanted to go even less. Much less, in fact.

With a heavy sigh, he decided he would wait a little longer. Wait and see. Talk to Bob. No need to jump and run yet. This might still come to nothing. Besides, he quite liked it here. He wasn't going to leave unless he really did have no choice.

Well, being realistic, he thought with a grimace, you always had a choice. In his case now, the choice might be between staying here and dying, or leaving and living for a bit longer. Some choice. If it came to that, of course. If things worked out badly.

'Your country?' he said when Magda returned to the terrace. 'Where's that, exactly?'

'Like I said, far from here.'

'I heard that,' he said with a wry smile. 'Does it have a name, this country of yours?'

'Česko, they want it to be called now. The Czech Republic. It used to be—'

'Part of Czechoslovakia.' He grinned and added, 'I collected stamps from there as a boy.'

'Stamps?'

'Postage stamps.'

When she still looked puzzled, he added impatiently, 'It doesn't matter. What's it like there these days?'

'Better, I think.'

'Than when you left?'

She nodded. 'Yes, I think so.'

'How long ago was that?'

'A few years, perhaps.'

"Perhaps"? What was that supposed to mean? He mulled it over.

'Where could I go there?'

She tossed her head and glared at him. 'You don't want me with you, just tell me! I will go somewhere else right now.'

'Don't be silly.' He sighed. 'It's dangerous to be with me, that's all. You don't need to put yourself in danger.'

'It is dangerous here already!' she said, eyes flashing. 'I know that. You know that. But I am here, aren't I?'

He nodded, her logic relentless, and too much for him. Then he smiled, wanting to reduce the tension between them. 'Do you know somewhere there where we could go – to stay?'

'Yes. I think so. There is a place in the country. An old cottage.' She shrugged. 'It is simple, very basic. But it will be safe there, I think.'

Perhaps. But was anywhere truly safe now? He doubted it.

'A cottage? You mean you have access to it – or what?'

She nodded again. 'It is simple,' she repeated. 'Not like here,' she added, with a gesture that took in the villa and its grounds, 'but maybe safer than staying here.'

That was almost certainly true, he thought with slightly more interest. Not absolutely safe, of course, but almost anywhere in the world would be safer than here now. Except North Korea, possibly.

They always said you had a better chance of losing yourself, and hiding out, in the anonymity of a big city. But he didn't like big cities, especially ones he didn't know, where every single person in the crowd could be the assassin hunting you. He preferred space and the open air. If someone was coming, he wanted to be able to see him, and know who he was. So big cities were out.

'Could we drive there?'

'Yes,' she said with a shrug. 'It would take a long time, but it is possible, I think.'

'How long?'

She frowned and did some mental arithmetic. 'Three days, perhaps.'

Not too bad. And a lot safer than going through airports or ferry terminals. It was something to consider, if things got worse – and if he ever got that desperate.

Provided, of course, Schengen survived the waves of migrants and asylum seekers sweeping across the continent at the moment. The general re-introduction of border controls would create problems for him, and probably for Magda, too. At present, the re-installed fences and security procedures were confined to countries facing south, but that could change at any moment.

'Maybe,' he said.

'Maybe we will go?'

He nodded.

Chapter 5

Fogarty got out of the car and stood gazing around for a few moments. The big, old farmhouse, built of Cotswold sandstone, looked wonderful in the gentle sunlight, and the view across the nearby meadows was even better. Open and, most importantly, boundary-free as far as the eye could see. A soft, warm breeze had the nearby beech trees rustling. He watched members of the resident colony of rooks squabbling and practising their aerobatics. Then his eyes turned to the man striding forward to meet him with outstretched arms: Mike Hendrik, his long-term chief of staff.

'All right, Ed?'

Fogarty grinned. 'Mike! How the hell are you?'

'It's me that should be asking that question, pal. I'm good. Never better. You?'

'Not too bad. And glad to be here.'

'The boys picked you up OK?'

Fogarty nodded. 'No complaints.'

They shook hands and hugged one another.

Hendrik gestured at their surroundings. 'It's not much of a place, I'm afraid, but I thought it would do for now. We've got it on a twelve months lease, not that we'll be staying that long.'

'It's perfect.' Fogarty glanced around with an appreciative eye. 'I can't go home, anyway,' he added with a grimace.

'Unfortunately,' Hendrik agreed. 'Come on! Let me show you around. We won't be here long, but you might as well know where things are – and what your money has bought. The journey OK, by the way?'

Fogarty nodded. 'Fine. As usual, your arrangements were perfect, Mike. Worked like a well-tuned machine.'

'Good to know.'

Hendrik steered him across the gravelled forecourt towards the open front door. 'You need to get some rest now, relax and then—'

'Fuck that! I ain't doing no more relaxing.' Fogarty scowled. 'I've just spent a year or more doing that. Now I want some action. There's a few accounts to be settled.'

'Lunch first, though?' Hendrik suggested with a grin.

Fogarty laughed and punched him playfully on the arm. 'That'll do for now!'

'So what's the plan?' Fogarty asked over the lunch table.

'I thought you might want to rest up here for a couple of days first, but it's up to you, of course. Then we leave by boat from the river. Meet up with the yacht well offshore. Head around the coast, maybe down to the Med.'

'Long term?'

Hendrik shrugged. 'We need to talk about that.'

Fogarty nodded. 'Makes sense. You've done well, getting everything organized like this.'

'You knew you could count on me, Ed.'

'Yeah.' Fogarty sighed. 'There were a few others I thought I could count on, as well. Like that bloody Nicci! More fool me.'

'Nicci!' Hendrik said, shaking his head. 'Who would have thought it?'

'Well, now it's payback time. We'll get to Nicci, but not straightaway. Let him stew a bit first.'

'He'll know you're out.'

'No doubt about that!' Fogarty gave a mirthless laugh. 'His new friends in the NCA – or SOCA, or whatever the hell it is now – will be sure to tell him, if he doesn't know already.

But some of the others can come first. Save the best for last. Who's going to be first?'

'The woman, I thought. Anna? She's in London.'

'Fine. Let's start with her. She won't have the money, though?'

'No.' Hendrik shook his head. 'She was nowhere near the money. But she said her piece at the trial.'

Fogarty nodded. 'I remember that. Bitch! She'll do for starters.'

He reflected for a moment or two and then added, 'I'm not letting the money go, though. We'll find it, and get it back, whatever it takes.'

'I thought you might say that. It's going to be tough, after all this time, but I think you're right.'

Hendrik frowned and added, 'We need it. A lot of properties and other assets have been seized while you've been away. Bank accounts frozen, and so on.'

'Not everything, though, surely?'

'Oh, no! Not everything – not yet, anyway. But no doubt they're still working on it.'

Fogarty grimaced.

'Something else you need to consider, Ed, is that good plastic surgery that's kept confidential doesn't come cheap.'

'Plastic surgery. I hate the idea of that,' Fogarty said with a shudder.

'Well, it may not be necessary. But if you want to live in this country, or most places in Europe, you should at least think about it.'

'That what you've been doing – thinking about plastic surgery?'

'Only some of the time!' Hendrik said with a grin. 'Myself, I'll probably be all right, but you...'

'I'm too well known,' Fogarty finished for him.

'That's about the size of it.'

Fogarty pondered for a moment and then shook his head. 'Fuck it! For now, at least. There's too much to do for me to be worrying about that.'

'Well, you'll be safe enough short-term, if we take care, but not long-term. You said it yourself. You're too well known. Where could you go? How could you live?'

The point was a good one. Fogarty accepted that. There were things to do here in the immediate future, but he couldn't spend the rest of his life chasing down vendettas. There had to be more to look forward to than that.

'So where do you suggest, Mike? Venezuela? The real bad boys always went to Argentina, didn't they?'

Hendrik shook his head. 'Venezuela's gone down the tubes economically, and in every other way as well. Argentina isn't much better. How about Cuba?'

'Cuba?'

'Things are starting to open up again there since Obama walked the walk, and talked to the Castros.'

Fogarty just stared at him.

Hendrik shrugged. 'Coca Cola will be in there, and McDonald's. All the usual corporate stuff. But so will the descendants of that financial guy the Mob had there back in the fifties. He laundered the money from the casinos for them – as well as the money from everywhere else.'

'Yeah. You're right,' Fogarty said, squinting through the smoke from his cigarette. 'Good accountant, Meyer. I wonder what happened to him.'

'He died. He reached a ripe old age in comfort and security, and then he died. I read about him.'

'Did he get to take his money with him?'

Hendrik grinned and shook his head. 'I don't think so. But the FBI never got it. Or him, either. He was good.'

Fogarty was silent for a few moments. Then he said speculatively, 'Cuba, eh? I've never thought about that.'

'Well, you should now. It's the coming place. A lot of people and money from Florida will be headed that way. No reason we shouldn't join them. I'm sure we'd find something to do there.'

Fogarty reached for the bottle of Rioja they had been enjoying over lunch and said, 'Tell me more.'

Chapter 6

Jake sat in the shadows next to the wall of the house and listened to the night. A breeze rustled the palm trees for a few moments and then died away again. An owl hooted mournfully. There was some rustling in the olive grove. His head turned sharply. Then he relaxed. He had no idea what was there, but the sound wasn't the kind that was a potential threat to him.

For another twenty minutes he stayed there, still and listening. Then he swore softly and shook his head. This was no good. He'd had no peace of mind since hearing from Bob. Jumping at nothing. Waiting for somebody to appear, probably in the middle of the night. It was too much. He couldn't go on like this. He had to do something. It made no sense to stay in the house, just waiting. He could do better than that.

There was Magda to consider, as well. This wasn't her fight. He didn't want to risk anything happening to her. Equally, he didn't want her to look after. Looking after himself would be more than enough. He just hoped he could do it. In the old days he had always worked alone. He was good at that, or had been once, and it was what he preferred. It was how he wanted it to be now.

So he had told Magda to return to the room he knew she still kept in the town.

'You are sending me away?' she said, looking and sounding both hurt and incredulous.

'It's for the best,' he told her. 'This isn't your fight.'

He winced as she turned her back on him and flounced out of the room.

For two days then he had the house to himself. On the first day, he busied himself making some preparations. They didn't amount to a hell of a lot, but he did what he could. He had to assume someone would come for him, and he had to be ready.

The gun he had always favoured, the Glock pistol, he kept close. Passport and money went into a small emergency bag he kept handy for quick collection on the way out. He rehearsed alternative escape routes, ready for an attack from different directions. His main vehicle, the all-wheel drive Honda SUV, he parked in a long-stay parking area on the edge of town, keeping only the battered old Ford pickup nearby as a runaround.

He satisfied himself that when – not if! – he had to leave, he would be able to do it quickly. A moment's notice would be all it would take. The first sign of trouble, and he would be gone.

On the third day he took the Ford truck and drove to meet Bob in Faro. It seemed sensible to wring what information he could out of the man who was supposed to be watching his back.

Fogarty might know he was in Portugal, even that he was in the Algarve, he reasoned as he drove towards Faro, but how could he possibly know where he lived? The Algarve was a big region. A couple of million people, at least, lived here. Unless Fogarty got lucky, they could spend the rest of their lives looking for him.

All he had to do was keep his head down, which was what he'd been doing for quite a while. All the same... He gave a crooked grin and shook his head. A lifetime was a long time to try to do that for.

Optimism always had been a problem, and sometimes

a danger, he thought ruefully. It encouraged laziness and wishful thinking. Best to assume they really did know where he lived.

Fogarty and co would know where he lived the same way they knew he was in Portugal. Someone had told them. Or they had access to information about him that somebody somewhere held. That was more likely.

So what had happened? It wasn't hard to think of an answer or two. One obvious possibility was Bob himself. Bob didn't need to have deliberately betrayed him. All he had to have done was keep a record on a computer. Perhaps that had even been required of him.

Everything was on a computer somewhere these days. Nobody in the world kept paper files and records anymore. If information was held at all, it was kept on a computer. And computer files could be hacked, and were hacked, by somebody – every sodding day of the year!

Another possibility was the financial arrangements made for him. It was naïve to believe that all that was known of him was his bank account number and a sort code. A manager or auditor responsible for overseeing pension payments wouldn't rest easy unless or until he knew more than that, and that sort of knowledge could be bought or forced from whoever possessed it.

So how Fogarty had discovered his whereabouts wasn't really much of a mystery at all. He didn't need to know the exact route they had followed. It was enough that Bob knew they had done it, and had told him so.

Thank you, Bob! Jake breathed. Forewarned was fore-armed. You might just have saved my life.

Chapter 7

'Who are they?' Fogarty asked.

'They're from Tenerife. They're good, I'm told.'

'Brits?'

Hendrik shrugged. 'They sound it, but who knows what anybody is these days? All I know is they come highly recommended.'

'Who by?'

'Rowlands.'

'The time-share guy?'

'That's the one.'

Fogarty chuckled and shook his head. 'Is he still in business?'

'I imagine so. He sounded full of himself the other week when I bumped into him in Ronnie Scott's.'

'So age hath not withered him?'

'Not much. Still a mean, little, nasty bastard.'

Fogarty chuckled some more and shook his head. 'Ronnie Scott's? I used to like that old place. What were you doing there? I didn't know you liked jazz.'

'I don't. Can't stand it, actually. I was looking for Rowlands. I'd been told he went there when he was in the UK.'

Fogarty nodded and opened the car window a couple of inches to let out some of the cigarette smoke.

'I thought I might have given these things up when I was inside,' he said ruefully, 'but there's not much else you can do in there. Except smoke, and think about things. Make promises to yourself about what you're going to do to the people who let you down, and betrayed you, when you get out.'

'No library?'

'Library!'

Fogarty choked himself laughing.

'A man could improve himself if he went to a library every day, you know, Ed.'

'Too late for that. But you're right. Maybe I could have been a brain surgeon.'

'In some ways, you already are.'

Fogarty laughed. He liked that. He laughed again as he thought about it. It was true. He'd re-arranged a few brains over the years.

'In some ways,' Hendrik reflected, changing the subject, 'I would rather we had our own specialists to take care of situations like this. Bringing in outsiders increases the risks.'

'We don't kill enough people,' Fogarty pointed out, still amused. 'Specialists would get bored, hanging around.'

'True.'

'Then what? Bored hitmen would be dangerous to have around the place. You would never know what they were going to do next to entertain themselves. Better this way. We've been through the pros and the cons on this before, haven't we?'

'Here she comes,' Hendrik said, bringing the small talk to an end.

She was on foot, walking from the Tube station half a mile away, carrying a plastic bag from a supermarket. Fogarty focused on her and scowled. He remembered her, all right. Bitch! Her performance in the witness box had done him no good at all.

'And that's them,' Hendrik said with satisfaction. 'Right behind, in the white Citroen.'

Fogarty watched with growing interest. He was curious to see how good these two really were.

The Citroen pulled up outside the house next door. The young woman with long blonde hair walked past it without a glance, fumbling in her bag for a key.

The driver, a young guy with a razor-cut hairstyle, got out of the car and just stood there, peering back along the street, keeping watch. He held the door half open, ready to dive back inside.

The passenger, also young and with the same hairstyle, got out. He walked quickly along the pavement, following the woman. As she reached the gate at the foot of the steps leading up to her front door, he seemed to call to her. Either that or she heard him coming. She stopped and turned round.

The passenger raised a pistol quickly and shot her. Twice, it looked like. A double-tap. She slumped to the pavement. The man closed in and fired twice more, making sure. When he straightened up and turned, the Citroen was already alongside him. He pulled the front passenger door open and folded himself inside easily. The car slid smoothly and quietly away. Within seconds it had turned a corner and was out of sight.

Hendrik started the engine of the van. He glanced at Fogarty. 'Satisfied?'

Fogarty nodded. 'Let's go.'

As they drove, Hendrik said, 'They looked pretty damn good to me. No fuss, no bother. Just in, and out. Smooth and fast. Job done.'

'Yeah. What about if somebody shoots back, though? How good are they then?'

Hendrik smiled. 'We'll have to see about that. Why? Are you thinking someone might shoot back?'

'Before we're finished? Who knows? But I can't believe they'll all go down as easily as she did.'

'Good point.'

Fogarty was thinking of the difference between a man with the only gun and the man who keeps his cool when everyone else has a gun as well. In his experience, it was a big difference. Still, he had to admit, what he had just seen was good. Mike had done well finding those two. They looked like a sharp and eager team.

'We'll do the next one ourselves,' Fogarty said.

Hendrik glanced at him, surprised.

'But keep the two young guys in reserve. And use them again. They're good.'

'Do it ourselves? What? You want to keep things tight?'

'Yeah. Besides, this is personal, remember?'

Hendrik nodded. It was. Of course it was. All the same, it wasn't what he had anticipated. 'We'll have to be careful,' he pointed out, 'if we're going to get directly involved.'

Fogarty nodded. 'Don't worry,' he said with a grim chuckle. 'It's not as if it will be the first time, is it?'

Hendrik didn't bother replying to that.

'So who do you want to go after next?' he asked instead.

Chapter 8

They met in a little café near the waterfront in Faro that they had used once before. Jake was there first this time. He sat and nursed a beer while he waited.

Bob arrived twenty minutes later, and shook his head when the waiter offered him a beer. He asked for coffee instead.

'No sign you were followed from the airport, I hope?' Jake said.

Bob shook his head. 'I went straight to my hotel, checked in and slipped out a back door. Picked up a cab on the street.'

'Risky. You didn't know who was picking you up.'

'Let's not overdo the paranoia, son. It's grim enough as it is. But if I see a bad guy coming this way, I'll let you know. OK?'

Jake grinned. 'Good to see you again, ol' timer!'

'And you. Where's that fucking coffee? I've had nowt to drink all day.'

'Easy, Bob. Did no-one tell you? We're very laid-back down here in the Algarve.'

'That's good, very good. I'll try to remember that. So should you, when I tell you what I know – and what I don't know.'

There it was, Jake thought. They'd got to the nub of the meeting in no time flat.

'It sounds bad.'

'Oh, it is bad!'

'So what happened? You told me Fogarty escaped and that he knew where to find me, but not much else.'

Bob sighed and looked up as the waiter returned with his coffee. Jake nodded when the waiter pointed at his near empty glass and looked at him expectantly.

Bob cleared his throat and said, 'You'd be better off with coffee than beer, Jake. You're going to have to keep your wits about you.'

'I'll be all right. Don't you worry about me.'

'I wish I didn't have to. He'll be coming for you, you know – for all of you, in fact. You do know that, don't you?'

Jake nodded. 'I've been expecting it.'

'Sooner, rather than later, I mean.'

'Let him come.' Jake shrugged. 'I'm not worried.'

'Well, you should be – especially now.'

'Why's that?'

Bob shrugged and gave a little grimace. 'More bad news, I'm afraid. I didn't want to tell you over the phone.'

'So tell me now.'

Jake stared hard, unblinking, knowing it was going to get worse.

Bob hesitated, as if uncertain how best to express himself. 'Anna,' he said with a sigh. 'That young lass from SOCA – remember her?'

Jake's pulse rate crept up. 'Go on,' he murmured, willing himself to stay calm.

'It looks like Fogarty got to her already. At least, somebody did. She was shot dead the other night.'

Jake grimaced. 'And you think it was him?'

'Him, or somebody acting for him.'

Jake shut up then while he absorbed the news. It was bad. So soon, too.

'What happened?'

'I don't know much.' Bob shrugged. 'Apparently, she went home after work in...'

'In London?'

'London, yes. That's right. She'd left SOCA and moved to the NCA quite recently. Anyway, she went home from work. Two men were waiting for her in a car. They got out and called her name after she walked past. When she turned round one of them shot her. She died instantly.'

Jake grimaced. 'There were witnesses, I take it?'

'Two or three. Ordinary folk. Neighbours. They said the gunman just shot her. Outside her own front gate, as well. Then him and his partner got back in the car and drove away. They didn't even wear balaclavas,' he added, shaking his head.

Professionals, Jake thought. A professional hit, an execution. They would probably be out of the country by now. Back to Moscow, or wherever. Sicily, maybe.

'She was a canny lass,' Bob said wistfully. 'She didn't have a lot to do with it, either. It's a damn shame.'

'People like Fogarty don't just scratch your car when they're out for revenge,' Jake pointed out.

Bob sighed, as if to say it was beyond his comprehension, despite all his policing years. Then he looked into his cup. 'I wouldn't mind another coffee. This cup's a bit small. I usually have a mug.'

'Jesus!' Jake glared at him, irritated by the trivial comment. Then he just shook his head. 'Get one,' he said. After a pause, he added softly, 'He's not going to get away with it, you know. Fogarty, I mean.'

'Let's hope not.'

'How did he get out, by the way? Anything more on that?'

'A helicopter came over the yard during the exercise hour, apparently, and opened up with a machine gun.'

'You're kidding!'

Bob shook his head. 'Opened fire – just like that. Didn't hit anyone, mind.'

'Surely they couldn't land it?'

'No. There's wires over the yard to stop that.'

'So what did they do – drop him a rope?'

'No. They just shot the place up, and flew off again. It was all over in twenty or thirty seconds.'

'A distraction?'

'That's right. When they did a count afterwards, Fogarty was gone.'

It wouldn't have been easy, Jake reflected, not even with all that mayhem going on. Belmarsh was a high security prison, as secure as anywhere in the country.

'So how did they do it?'

'They coerced a few prison officers. Took their families hostage and told them what would happen if they didn't get Fogarty through the security doors. Left it to them to work out how to do it.'

'He's good at that sort of thing.' Jake shook his head, remembering. 'What else did he do – send them their kids' ears and fingers?'

'The wives were beaten up – badly – and then they gave them photographs of their faces.'

Jake grimaced and shook his head. That would work. It nearly always did.

'On the phone you mentioned Nicci. What about him?'

'Aye. Nicci, and the others.' Bob shrugged and added, 'All of you, really. You're all in the same boat now. Yourself, of course, you're different to the others, but still...'

'Different? In what way?'

'Well, you could do something about it. None of the others can. They don't have the capability.'

'I'm not so sure about that,' Jake said with a wry smile. 'Have you warned everybody, by the way?'

Bob shook his head. 'I don't even know where they are, not now.'

'For chrissake! They're in witness protection. I thought you were supposed to keep tabs on them?'

'That's right. We are.' Bob shrugged. 'We tried to keep an eye on them. It started off OK. Then they slipped off the radar.'

Jake wondered what that meant. He wasn't impressed.

'What did they do – go back to their original identities?'

'Some did.'

'Stupid buggers!'

'It's hard, you know. Not everyone can handle a lifetime of exile from friends, family and the places they know. And getting used to a name that's not yours can be a problem, as well.'

'Better than being dead!'

'Yeah.'

Despite his reaction, Jake could understand all that. It was one reason why he had declined the offer of witness protection himself, although what he'd opted for wasn't a lot different in practice. Looking after himself the way he had been doing amounted to a life in exile, even if he was in charge of it himself.

'We do our best for them,' Bob resumed, 'but... Well, there it is. We are where we are. What I want you to do now, Jake, is find them. Find the others, and warn them. Give them a chance to get clear.'

'Me?' Jake chuckled. 'Why me?'

'Because I think you can do it. That's why.'

Jake shook his head. 'No way! I'm not doing it. I've got enough to do looking after myself.'

'Oh, I think you will. Otherwise, you're not the man I've always thought you were.'

Jake swore and grumbled for a minute or two more. Bob waited patiently.

'What about your lot? The cops – or the security services, for that matter? What are they going to do?'

'The security services have got their hands full with today's problems. And we in the police are not up to it. It's as simple as that. By the time we get organized, and find out from the lawyers what we're allowed to do these days, you'll probably all be dead. We'll be left to organize press conferences, express our condolences to the families and ship the bodies home.'

'So we're on our own,' Jake said bitterly. 'All the help you got from us for that trial, and then when the wheels come off we're on our own?'

'I just wish I could tell you different, son.'

Jake knew that would be right. Bob wouldn't be proud of the position he found himself in. But he was a realist. He was here because he felt something could be done, and should be done. There were lives that could be saved.

Experimentally, he manoeuvred his half-full glass into line with the empty one and Bob's coffee cup. It didn't look right. The line was top-heavy at one end. He fiddled a bit more, but he knew it was hopeless. It couldn't be done, however much he wanted it to be done. But he had to keep on trying.

He looked up at Bob and with a weary sigh said, 'So what do you want me to do?'

Chapter 9

When Bob announced that he'd had nothing to eat all day they moved on to a little restaurant Jake knew.

'Nothing all day?' Jake said. 'What? You were flying cargo class?'

Bob scowled. 'They don't do proper meals any more, most airlines. It's got like the railways.'

'Nothing to eat?'

'Just bits and pieces, toasties and things, stuff that looks better in the photos than on your plate. Well, you don't get a plate any more, either. It's just wrapped up in cellophane and cardboard.'

'And there was me,' Jake said, 'thinking motorway service areas are the pits.'

Bob shook his head. 'Not at all. You can get hot meals there, proper meals.'

'Come on, old timer!' Jake said, grinning. 'Let's find a restaurant, and get some decent food into you.'

But it didn't get a lot better in the restaurant Jake chose, or with the meal he ordered in Portuguese for them both.

'Sardines?' Bob said, when the meal came.

'Yeah. They're a local specialty.'

'Sardines,' Bob said again, staring at his plate.

'It's a healthy meal. Try it.'

'Healthy? If you say so,' Bob said with resignation.

They started eating. Jake tried to recall where they had got to in their discussion.

Then something that had been bothering him in the background came to the fore of his mind.

'You haven't just found out, have you, Bob?'

'Found out what?'

'About the others vanishing. You've known for a while, haven't you?'

'A little while, yes.'

'What happened?'

Bob sighed and put down his knife and fork. 'About the leak, you mean?'

Jake nodded. 'The leak, and the chronology.'

'What you have to understand, Jake, is that until a couple of years ago everything to do with witness protection was in the hands of the country's individual police services. That's how it was when all this started. So far as the Northumbria Police Service was concerned, it was down to me to see that these people were looked after. It was my responsibility. No-one else's.

'Then the government went and created the National Crime Agency, and they made it responsible for the national coordination of witness protection. Now the NCA may turn out to be a good thing eventually – I don't deny it – but giving them control of witness protection has increased the possibilities of leakage. More people are in the know. It's as simple as that.'

Jake mulled it over for a moment. 'And the information is no doubt all on paperless files somewhere?'

'On computers? Yes, of course it is.'

Jake sighed. 'And given that a teenage anorak can hack into the American missile launch codes...'

'I know, I know! Exactly.'

'And that's progress?'

'So they say.'

'Marvellous, bloody marvellous!'

Bob nodded and looked grim-faced. 'Face it, Jake. We may never know how, where or when the leak occurred.

And all we know right now is that the files were illegally accessed.'

'So – let me guess – you decided to warn Nicci and the others that this had happened. They listened to you, and then they each decided they would rather look after their own security in future? Is that how it went?'

'Pretty well. One by one, they dropped out of sight and disappeared.'

'Can't say I blame them.'

'No. Neither can I.' Bob sighed. 'It gives us a problem, though. We're still charged with protecting them.'

'Mm.'

'You were lucky,' Bob reflected. 'Lucky or well advised.'

'You think?'

'Well, you declined the offer of witness protection, didn't you?'

'I didn't see any need for it. I wasn't involved for very long, and I didn't get in very deep anyway. I doubted Fogarty even knew I existed.'

'Oh, he knows all right! And he'll have been looking for you. But at least nobody could leak your whereabouts to him. You weren't on file. So nobody knew.'

'Except you.'

'Except me. And nobody has offered me money yet for the information,' Bob added with a grin.

Jake smiled. He trusted Bob with his life. He'd done that already.

'I don't feel lucky,' he said with feeling. 'I could have avoided all this if I'd been sensible, and said no to you in the first place.'

'We could all say that. That's the road not travelled, isn't it?'

'Yeah.'

'It doesn't matter much now anyway, Jake. Somehow Fogarty found out. And we've heard that he knows you're out here in Portugal.'

'From informants? That how you've heard?'

'Yeah.'

'It's amazing you've got any informants left. What's the matter with them? Are they all daft?'

'Poor or greedy, mostly. They do it for the money, the same reason most of us do things.'

'You're just full of insights into human nature, Bob. You're wasted in your job.'

'Aye. You're right.'

'OK,' Jake said, trying to pull things together. 'Let's go through the cast, and see what you know. You mentioned Nicci. Where's he, for a start?'

'Nikos Antonakis. Initially, he disappeared into the Greek community in London. We knew where he was for a time. Then he just vanished.'

'You were paying him, presumably?'

'We were, and we are still. But the account we pay into hasn't been accessed for a while.'

'Maybe he's dead?'

Bob shook his head. 'We don't think so. His body would have been found. Fogarty would have wanted his body to be found. No, he's gone underground – in the nicest possible way.'

Might be better to leave him there, Jake thought. In the circumstances. Safer, anyway. Nicci was good. As well as being a nice enough guy, even if he was a crook, he was clever financially. He would have worked something out for himself. He certainly knew what to expect if Fogarty caught up with him. He would do anything to avoid that.

He sighed and said, 'Nicci could be anywhere.'

'Anywhere,' Bob agreed. 'He could. You're right. But my guess is he's gone home.'

'Home? Greece, you mean?'

Bob nodded. 'Crete, actually, where he came from as a boy with his parents. The family will have stayed in touch with the old country, and Nicci will no doubt have been back there many times, visiting.'

'Have you looked there for him?'

Bob shook his head. 'Not really. We've made inquiries, but nothing has come of them yet.'

'If you can't locate him, maybe Fogarty won't be able to, either.'

'It doesn't work like that, though, does it? Fogarty will buy or torture the information out of somebody. There could be a trail of bodies leading all the way to Nicci.'

Jake grimaced. True enough. Fogarty, he thought, shaking his head again.

'Then there's Walter Penrose,' Bob said. 'He's somewhere in Yorkshire, I believe. Leeds, probably.'

'Has he gone home, as well?'

'Near enough.'

'Jack Gregory?'

'No idea. The last I heard of him, he was in the north of Scotland somewhere.'

Jake sighed and pushed his plate away. 'You're not giving me very much, Bob. What the hell do you expect me to do?'

'Find 'em,' Bob said with a steely look. 'Do what you used to be good at. Intelligence, wasn't it? Spying?'

'A long time ago,' Jake said with a sigh. He thought about it, frowned and added, 'There was another woman involved, as well as Anna, wasn't there? I never met her, but I knew she was around. I heard her mentioned.'

Bob nodded. 'That was Petra Voyshenko. Russian, I believe. She wasn't with us, though.'

'She was on the other side? With Fogarty, you mean?'

'Something like that.'

'So where is she now? Back in Moscow?'

'Probably.'

'What about Freddie?'

'Still in London, as far as we know. Maybe you should start with him.'

'Maybe I should.'

They talked some more, without getting a lot further. Jake

absorbed the scant extra information Bob handed over, and made a few notes. But it didn't amount to much, and it wasn't a hell of a lot to work with. He was going to have to do most of the spadework himself.

Frankly, he felt like simply disappearing, and letting them all get on with it. That was still an option for him. Why should it be down to him to find and warn the others? They hadn't been friends, or even colleagues, for long. Some of them, like Nicci, were career criminals anyway. Why the hell was Bob tasking him with finding them?

What he suspected was that Bob, or the senior people behind him, had hoped that in the process of looking he would find Fogarty for them. Or, if not that, Fogarty would come out of hiding to get him. So he would be live bait.

He gave a mirthless grin. Alive for now, at least.

'There is one other thing,' Bob said finally. 'I don't know if you know this, but the haul from that job was never fully recovered.'

'No?'

'We got part of it, but a big lump stayed missing. Even more reason for Fogarty to be looking for his former colleagues. He'll think one of them must have it.'

'How much is missing?'

'Twenty million, give or take a million or two.' Bob grinned at him and added, 'I wouldn't be surprised if Fogarty really wants to talk to the van driver about that – if nothing else!'

'Go on, Bob. Cheer me up.'

Chapter 10

He didn't blame Bob, Jake decided on the drive back to São Brás. It wasn't Bob's fault. The witness protection scheme had been a good option for turncoats, and for agents who had been working long-term undercover, in some cases for several years, and then had had to appear in their true colours in open court. Something had to be done to protect people like that. Now, though? Well, now it seemed like a disaster, a total fuck-up, a reminder that if things can go wrong, they probably will.

Staying out of it hadn't helped him much, either, he thought grimly. He was in the same boat as the others now anyway. Somehow names and locations, including his, had leaked. No doubt money had changed hands to make that happen. And now Fogarty was out, they were all seriously at risk. Every single one of them. Anyone who had ever stood against Fogarty knew what to expect.

Bob didn't know the source of the leak, and now he was paddling like hell trying to keep them all afloat. He probably wished he'd taken the retirement package when it was offered a couple of years ago, instead of getting involved in this sorry business. He'd certainly had enough years behind him. Instead, he'd fancied taking one last crack at a Mr Big. And look where it had got him!

Where he did blame Bob, though, was for involving him. That had come about because they had known each other personally, and once had even worked together briefly. So, naturally, Bob had thought of him when he needed an extra man from outside the Northumbria service for a short time. Naturally. And look how well that had worked out!

If only he hadn't been bored out of his skull at the time, and eager to do anything to get the adrenaline flowing again. If only. He gave a grim smile and shook his head.

The job had been to stop the heist and bring Fogarty down. The cops in the Met, as well as in a few other places, were sick to death of him getting away with things they knew for certain were down to him. He'd been doing it for years. Only clever, mercenary lawyers and intimidated and murdered witnesses had kept him out of prison and in his Essex mansion. So when inside information about the proposed job came along, it had looked like the opportunity the police had been awaiting a long time.

The job had been straightforward enough. A cash heist, the sort of thing Fogarty had specialized in for many years. As so often, Nicci the Greek had set this one up for him. A cash centre in the Team Valley, Gateshead, one of thirty dotted around the country as part of the Bank of England's Note Circulation Scheme (NCS). The centres stored banknotes and distributed them to, and collected them from, retailers and financial institutions, ATMs and so on, as needed.

They were operated by four or five private companies – retail banks and security firms – that were the members of the NCS at the time. It was a system that had been introduced in 2001 to reduce the burden on the Bank of England, and the risk, of moving banknotes long distances around the country. It was up to the members of the NCS to make sure they were adequately protected by insurance.

Jake had been surprised to learn that despite internet retailing and the seemingly universal use of plastic, cash retained a massive role in the economy. In fact, there were more banknotes in circulation in the UK than ever before: £64 billions' worth in 2015.

He had also been intrigued to learn that the NCS cash centres were home to eye-watering piles of banknotes at any time, and even more so in the run-up to Christmas, and afterwards for the January sales. The cash mountains reach a peak around February, by which time the shopping has eased off, and an awful lot of banknotes are coming home to rest until they are next needed.

The Team Valley cash centre had banknotes worth £40 million when Fogarty hit it late one dreary February evening. The gang didn't completely empty the place but it wasn't for want of trying, and there wasn't much left when they departed.

Fogarty had well-established systems for laundering the cash take from jobs, systems that had served him well over the years. Nicci again. So cash could be moved quickly and efficiently, and a good price obtained for it. Used banknotes were especially valuable.

Something else that was attractive about Nicci's proposal, from Fogarty's point of view, was that it was in an area where they weren't used to crimes of such magnitude. They had never had one. And it was well away from the territory of the Met, Fogarty's main adversary for so many years.

All in all, the job should have been safe, easy and lucrative. So it would have been, too, without the undercover team that the Met had worked into the heart of Fogarty's operation, and if Nicci hadn't been attracted by the offer of a clean slate in exchange for collaboration.

From the cops' point of view, the main objective was to catch Fogarty at it. It was no good arresting only the hired help. They wanted the man himself. Otherwise, he would walk away again, and live to fight another day. His lawyers would contend that what his employees did in their spare time was up to them. It was nothing to do with him.

Over the years it had been no good thinking the hired help could be turned. Fogarty rewarded his people handsomely if they took it on the chin when they were caught. They always knew that they, and their families, would be well looked after if they stayed loyal. As for anybody who sold out, well, it was likely to be a short life with a painful and distressing end.

That was how it had always been. But the game changer this time was that Nicci had been turned. Somehow. They had him on toast. He had to cooperate.

Nicci persuaded Fogarty, against his usual practice and better judgement, to be in on the heist personally. He sensed Fogarty wanted to feel the old adrenaline rush once again, before he got too old for it. Mike Hendrik argued against it, but Nicci was persuasive and Fogarty was hooked. Gateshead was safe, Nicci insisted. Nothing was going to happen there. They would be in and out fast, with nobody hurt or left behind. The local cops would all be asleep. The Met were 300 miles away.

Jake came into it late in the day. One of the getaway drivers broke his leg playing Sunday league football for his local pub team. They needed a replacement. Nicci said he would find one. He talked to Bob, his local contact in the Northumbria police, who came up with Jake. Jake, bored to death in premature retirement from the secret service, jumped at the opportunity. So that's how it was, going into the job.

But confusion reigned that February evening. More than one police service was involved, for a start. So there were communication and liaison problems. Then the inside team had needed to keep their heads down in the final run-up, to avoid suspicion and to make sure the job went ahead. An unfortunate result was that the main police effort was focused on nearby premises where banknotes for governments around the world were printed, rather than the NCS cash centre where sterling banknotes were stored.

Unbelievable. You couldn't have made it up. But that's what happened.

So when Jake drove one of the getaway vans around the corner, exactly as planned, his arrival at a police cordon created consternation. The plan had been to stop the raid in its tracks, before the gang got inside the cash centre. The way things actually developed, though, improvisation was needed to stop the raiders escaping with what they had come for.

That went surprisingly well. A Met back-up team hastily re-deployed made the stop, and believed they had caught the whole lot of them, Fogarty included. His lawyers screamed entrapment and provocation at the trial, but for once they were pissing into the wind. They got nowhere. And Fogarty got thirty years.

All the informants and undercover people on the heist, and Nicci especially, were marked for life, of course. They all knew that. They had known from the outset. So arrangements were made for them to build new lives under the witness protection scheme.

That should have been good enough. Seemingly, it hadn't been.

And this is what it had come to, Jake thought with a sigh. Well, he would just have to deal with it. And the others would have to look after themselves. Every man for himself, whatever Bob wanted. It was all right Bob talking heroically, but it wasn't his life that was on the line.

As for Nicci? Oh, he'd liked Nicci well enough, as he'd come to know him, but Nicci was a career criminal. He didn't owe him, or anyone else in the undercover team, one damn thing. He hadn't even met some of them before the trial.

Besides, realistically, what could he do that the country's police forces, especially the Met, couldn't do? Bob was being ridiculously naïve.

None of them needed warning anyway. They knew what danger they were in. They always had known. That's why they'd fled from witness protection. And, now, they would know soon enough that Fogarty had escaped from prison. It would be all over the papers and the TV screens. Millions of opinions shared on Facebook and Twitter, as well, no doubt.

No way, he thought, shaking his head. Get real, Bob! Thanks for the warning, but I'm out of it – and I'm staying out. If I can't do that here, in São Brás, I'll move on. I might even go to see what that cottage Magda was on about looks like. Why not? It's an option.

Then something else struck him. Somebody, somewhere, must know what had happened to the twenty million pounds, mostly in used banknotes, that was apparently still missing from the heist.

That was an interesting thought.

Chapter 11

They sent people to rummage around Palmers Green, Wood Green, Chelsea, and the other areas in London popular with Greeks, but nothing came of it. The few who recognized the name or the face of Nicci simply shrugged and said they had no idea where he was now. Gone away, probably. They hadn't seen him for years, months anyway.

It wasn't a stone wall they were facing; it was more a wall of indifference bred of lack of knowledge. Nobody seemed to know enough even to be curious, let alone to be worried about the questions. Nobody knew anything. It was a dead end.

'We're asking in the wrong places,' Fogarty said, swirling scotch over the ice cubes in his glass.

'You think?'

Fogarty nodded.

Hendrik weighed it up. 'Maybe,' he admitted, 'but our boys generally know where to go.'

'Then they're not asking the right people.'

'So what do you suggest?'

'Get your coat, Mike. I fancy a Greek meal. Haven't had one of them for a long time.'

Hendrik stared at him. 'All the trouble we've gone to, and you want to risk throwing it all away by appearing in public? You're mad!'

'Get your coat!' Fogarty chuckled. 'Let's go and have a bit of fun.'

They visited a restaurant where Fogarty had once been well known, and quite a favoured customer. That was before his arrest, and long before he ever saw the inside of Belmarsh. Now it was different. From the moment he set foot inside the place, it was different.

Hendrik was worried by all the eyes that sought them out.

'Christ, we can't stay here, Ed!'

Fogarty ignored him and headed straight for the table he had always preferred. He plonked himself down on a chair and turned his head to take in the restaurant. Hendrik hesitated a moment or two before joining him. When one of the waiters noticed them, realized who they were and backed off, he almost got up again.

'Ed, they'll be on the phone to the cops.'

Fogarty shook his head. 'Not if they've got any brains.'

Smiling, he beckoned one of the waiters over. 'Tell the boss I want to see him. And bring us a bottle of good wine – a good one, mind! None of your house rubbish.'

The man smiled nervously and ducked his head before scurrying away.

Hendrik tapped his fingers on the table anxiously, and wondered if he should have the car brought to the front door right now. They couldn't stay. He knew that. This was crazy.

'Mr Fogarty!' Costa, the owner, cried as he came bustling towards them. 'How are you? Long time since you are here.'

'Too true, Costa. But it's not my fault. Circumstances detained me.'

'And now you are free? Wonderful! Let me bring you our special menu.'

As Costa bustled away, Fogarty winked at Hendrik and said, 'Relax, Mike.'

'You stupid sod!' Hendrik responded, grinning reluctantly. 'If the Met still had a Flying Squad, they would be here by now.'

Fogarty shrugged. 'Life is full of "ifs". You can't allow yourself to be deflected by them.'

Costa returned, and helped them with a small menu he kept for favoured customers. As they chose, he congratulated them on their choice, and ushered in a wine waiter with a very special bottle.

'One thing I want to ask you, Costa,' Fogarty said as they finished ordering. 'Nicci – that is, Nikos Antonakis. Have you seen him recently, or heard of him?'

'Nicci?' Costa screwed up his face as he concentrated and tried to recall if he knew anything. 'Antonakis? No, I don't know about him. Not for a long time.'

'Think, Costa, think!' Fogarty urged. 'And when you remember something, let me know, huh?'

'Of course, Mr Fogarty.'

Fogarty leant back in his chair and looked around. 'Nice place, you have here.'

'Thank you,' Costa said nervously. 'Yes, it is. Very nice, I think.'

'I hope you have good insurance for it – fire insurance, for instance?'

Costa nodded slowly, seeing where this was headed.

'And loss-of-business insurance, of course. That's important. If anything happened here, you'd need that while the rebuilding took place – or until you could get another place sorted out. You couldn't afford to be shut for six months, could you? The bills would keep on coming, even if the money didn't. And meanwhile staff and customers would disappear like spring snow.'

'Insurance?' Costa repeated weakly, as if it were a novel idea.

Fogarty shook his head and looked at Hendrik. 'What do you think, Mike?'

'Can you get that kind of insurance? Insurance that's good enough, I mean?'

'I don't know. It's a question.' Fogarty sighed and looked around speculatively. 'Mario? What do you think?'

After a long pause, Costa said with resignation, 'I did hear he'd gone back to the old country.'

'Who did?' Fogarty said, looking puzzled.

'Antonakis.'

'Ah!'

'Where's that?' Hendrik asked innocently. 'The old country?'

'Greece.'

'Oh? Where, exactly?'

Costa shrugged despondently. 'One of the islands, possibly. I don't really know.'

With one finger, Fogarty reached out and tipped the special bottle of wine off the table. It fell with a crash onto the stone floor. A wave of red wine swept around Costa's feet, making him step back hurriedly.

'You'll have to do better than that,' Fogarty said gently.

Costa glared at him and then spun round to call one of the waiters, who were all looking to see what had caused the commotion. A young man came over. Costa spoke to him fast.

'In English,' Fogarty snapped.

'Attis, these gentlemen wish to know where Nikos Antonakis is from in Greece. You know, I believe?'

The waiter looked at all three of them, seemed to understand the situation and said, 'Crete. He is from Crete.'

'Thank you, Attis,' Fogarty said. He pushed back his chair and stood up.

Hendrik rose with him and said, 'Sorry about the wine, Costa.'

Costa gave him a thin smile, a little bow and an unspoken message: Go on, get the fuck out of here!

Then the young waiter, inexperienced in such matters, snarled with contempt and said something that didn't need translation to be understood.

Fogarty paused for a moment. Then he turned and reached out. He grabbed the waiter by a bunch of his shirt front, smashed him in the belly with his fist, and head-butted him savagely. The waiter sagged, broken. Blood spurted from where his nose used to be.

Costa reached out automatically. Hendrik, even quicker, seized his arm and stopped him.

'Tell him to apologize,' Fogarty said.

Costa steadied himself and spoke to the waiter, who gasped and mumbled in return.

'In English,' Fogarty snapped.

'I apologize,' the waiter whispered without further prompt.

Fogarty studied him a moment longer and then let go of his shirt front. 'You'd better mean it,' he warned before turning to head for the exit.

Chapter 12

Hendrik followed Fogarty outside, out into the blessedly busy street where no-one took any notice of them. He began to relax.

'So that's where Nicci is,' Fogarty mused as they walked back to the car parked a couple of blocks away. 'Crete, eh?'

Hendrik nodded. 'Sounds right.'

'Yeah. It had to be somewhere like that. It's a big island, though.'

'We'll find him, if he's there.'

'He will be.'

'You think?'

'Not much doubt about it.' Fogarty grinned. 'Twenty million quid on Crete? We'll soon spot him. He'll be living like a fucking king!'

'He could do that in London.'

'Until we caught up with him.'

They reached the car, opened the doors and climbed inside. Hendrik paused a moment, thinking about Nicci.

Fogarty motioned impatiently. 'Come on! Let's get moving before the cops arrive. Costa's courage will have returned now we've left.'

Hendrik chuckled and started the engine.

Crete, Fogarty thought. Went there once, a long time ago. Who was it with? Angie? Yeah.

Angie. Can't remember much about it, though. Holidays

were always spent in an alcoholic daze back then. Sex daze, as well, with Angie!

The only thing he'd always avoided was the drugs. Fool's holiday, that game. Eat 'em, smoke 'em, sniff 'em – it always came to the same thing in the end. He should know. He'd seen plenty of it. Too many old pals had succumbed. Quite a few people he'd known who weren't old pals, as well.

Maybe he should have stuck with Angie, he thought moodily. In many ways, she was the best of them – the women he'd had, the wives, the girlfriends. None of them had lasted. Couldn't stand the life, or else he'd got so he couldn't stand them. But Angie had lasted longer than most. She'd been just about the best looking, too.

Ah, well! Such was life. In the end, you were better off with cash and good pals. Mike, for instance. That was the real winning combination. Never mind the women. You could always buy them.

'Do we know anybody with links out there, Mike?'

'Crete?' Hendrik shook his head. 'Don't think so. But I can check around.'

'Might be worth it. Meanwhile, let's find one of the other traitors. Fat Freddie, for instance. Is he in London still?'

'Oh, yes! I would think so. Fat Freddie won't be far away.'

'If we find him living in style, we'll know we don't need to go to Crete.'

Hendrik chuckled. 'Freddie living in style? That would be a first!'

'Who else is there?'

'Well,' Hendrik said, considering, 'there's Penrose in Yorkshire, and Gregory somewhere in Scotland.'

Fogarty thought for a moment and then shook his head. 'Neither of them had the brains to get the money. They still need sorting, though. Find them. Once you know where they are, send those two lads from Tenerife.'

'Right. I'll get on it.'

'Anyone else?'

'Apart from Freddie?' Hendrik shook his head slowly. 'Just Nicci, really.'

Fogarty nodded and adopted a judicious expression. 'Crete, eh? I suppose it always was going to be Nicci. Someone smart, quick on his feet and good with money.'

'Well,' Hendrik said thoughtfully, 'either him or the guy he hired at the last minute to drive one of the vans. He's in the Algarve.'

'Oh, yes! I was forgetting about him. They brought him in as a witness as well, didn't they? The Algarve?'

Hendrik nodded. 'So I'm told. He's been there a while now. A small town in the hills.'

Fogarty wiped condensation off the side window and peered out into what was becoming a wet night. He listened to the wipers click-clacking across the windscreen. One of them needed replacing. Every now and then it stuck a bit and squeaked.

'Quite a night,' Hendrik ventured, peering ahead through the gloom. 'And getting even wetter.'

'Yeah. What did you say his name was?'

'Who?'

'That guy in the Algarve.'

'Ord, Jake Ord.'

'Jake Ord,' Fogarty repeated, trying to recall what the guy had looked like in the witness box. He shook his head, giving it up.

'Him next, maybe?' Hendrik suggested.

'Why not?'

Hendrik nodded and switched the wipers on to a higher speed, thinking maybe they would get better weather in the Algarve. Better than this, anyway.

'Then we'll come back for Fat Freddie,' Fogarty said.

'And after that we could go to Crete, and wrap it up.'

'Sounds like a plan,' Fogarty said complacently, stretching and yawning.

Chapter 13

Jake stopped the truck well short of the villa, hesitated a few moments and then set off to walk the last few hundred yards. Was it caution, or precaution? Paranoia even? He didn't know. He didn't know the difference, or even if there was one.

All he knew was that it was time to trust no-one, and to be very, very careful. The news about the woman in London, Anna, was proof enough of that. But he'd known anyway. The meeting with Bob had only served to underline the danger he faced.

Although it was dark, he knew the area well enough to use a local path that ran through the olive groves surrounding the villa. Underfoot it was hard earth, dust and dead grass. No twigs or branches to trip him up, or for him to step on noisily.

It was a quiet evening. An owl passed by overhead. He heard the beat of its wings as it gave itself a little extra power in order to hover. There were bats, too. Plenty of them. He could hear them squeaking as they whipped through the night air and went about their foraging. Cicadas, as well. He could hear them all around as he made his way between the olive trees.

The warm, humid air was heavy with the scent of late summer. He could smell the dry, dead grass and the patches of bare earth, where the season had taken its toll. There was a heady fragrance coming from a nearby orchard and from the jasmine bush close to the front door of the villa. The scent of the earth, and all its fruits.

And something else. He froze.

At the first whiff of cigarette smoke he stopped dead, all his senses on high alert. Close to the trunk of an ancient olive tree, heart beating fast, he stood absolutely rigid. He listened hard for minutes on end, but heard nothing out of the ordinary at all. The cigarette smoke faded.

Maybe nothing? Someone passing by on the road, perhaps. Or one of his neighbours out for a stroll around his property. He couldn't recall seeing any of them smoking, but no doubt some of them had the habit still.

If it was cigarette smoke? It was. He was sure of that, at least. What he wanted was an explanation.

Slowly, he raised an arm and wiped his face with his shirt sleeve. It was hot. God, so hot! He was dripping, the sweat running down his face, the sodden shirt clinging to his back.

He tried to ignore the discomfort and concentrate. It was difficult. This was the wrong place to be on a night like this. He should be in the house, behind the fly screens, safe from the mosquitoes. This was purgatory.

He was almost ready to move, about to tell himself he probably hadn't really smelled cigarette smoke, when he heard someone, a man, not very far away clear his throat.

He stiffened at the sound and focused hard again. Stealthily, he began to move sideways, circling around the location where the noise had come from. He knew now where the smoker, the throat clearer, was. He was on the terrace outside the villa.

Who was it, though? He was so intent on trying to assess who was there that he tripped and almost fell when he heard a voice, a male English voice, coming from a different direction altogether.

'How much longer do we have to wait?'

'It could be a while yet. Now shut up! Keep quiet, and

be patient. Listen to the mosquitoes, and marvel at their intricate fucking lifestyle.'

'Fuck 'em! Fuck you, as well.'

'Nice.'

Jake had heard enough.

They were waiting for him. Men sent by Fogarty were here, and no doubt ready to put a bullet in his head once they had satisfied themselves that he really didn't know where the missing £20 million was.

He edged back the way he had come, heart still thumping but in control. Bad as the situation was, at least the danger was tangible now. He no longer had to worry he was just fantasizing. The threat was real. He could do something about that.

By the time he reached the truck, he had worked out what he was going to do. He started the engine, turned and headed for the car park where he had left the Honda. It was time to get out. It was also time he talked to Magda again.

Chapter 14

She was startled to see him when she opened the door to her single room, bedsit apartment, but she quickly recovered her poise.

'Jake! Everything is all right?'

He shook his head. 'Are you alone?'

'Of course. Something has happened?'

'I've got to get out of here. You, as well, Magda. There were men waiting for me at the villa. They will kill me, if they can.'

'Oh!' Her hand flew to her mouth. 'Me, too?'

'I'm sorry.' He shrugged. 'But if they know where I live, they will also know about you. They will use you to get at me.'

'I understand.'

'You don't!' he snapped, impatient with her apparent calmness. 'You can't possibly. But we've got to leave tonight – now, in fact!'

'Now? Where will we go, Jake?'

'I don't know.' He shook his head. 'That doesn't matter. Just collect your stuff. Not everything – just what you need, and what you don't want to leave behind. That is...' He hesitated before adding, 'If you want to come with me?'

'I am your woman,' she said, touching his face tenderly with her finger tips. 'And you are my man. I will come.'

They were out of the apartment a quarter of an hour later. It wasn't a minute too soon so far as Jake was concerned.

He took a couple of the bags Magda had hurriedly packed, hoping she had included only things that would be useful.

He had very little himself. Just what was in his pockets and the emergency bag that he had transferred from the truck to the car. The important stuff. Nothing else really mattered. It could all be replaced. There had been a time when he was used to travelling light. He could do it again.

As Magda closed and locked the door to her apartment, he wondered if she would see it again. For that matter, he wondered if he would ever return to the villa. Fuck it, he thought. It's a house. That's all. And this is just a room in an apartment block made of concrete. Nothing to get sentimental about.

'Ready?' he asked, as she turned to face him.

She nodded. Then they left.

Magda waited until they were in the Honda, the engine started, before asking again, 'Where will we go, Jake?'

'I'm not sure. Let's just get moving.'

She placed her hand on his arm as he put the car in gear. 'I have an idea, in that case,' she said calmly.

'Oh?'

He pulled out into the street and headed towards the roundabout at the top of the Avenida.

'I know somewhere we can go,' she said quietly.

He took a moment, thinking about it.

'How far is it?'

'Maybe one hour.'

He had nothing to suggest. So he just nodded. All that mattered was getting out of here.

'OK. How do we get there?'

'Go to the next roundabout, and then take the turning to Alportel. I will navigate.'

He glanced sideways and forced a smile for her. 'I knew there was a good reason I invited you along!'

Now they were moving, now they were out of town, he began to feel slightly easier. Not relaxed. Far from it. Disaster could be around any corner, or could come up fast from behind at any moment, headlights blazing. Running away wasn't much of an answer, but it was better than the alternative.

They drove up into the hills, staying on the EN2 as far as Barranco do Velho. Jake drove as fast as he could sensibly manage on the intricately winding road, taking the corkscrew bends first one way and then the other, keeping an eye on the rear view mirror. Pursuit began to seem unlikely but he was past worrying about whether or not he was being paranoid.

'Nothing?' Magda said, seeing him glance at the mirror yet again.

He shook his head. 'Unless they were watching your place, as well as mine, there's no reason for them to be following us.'

She nodded.

At Barranco they turned west, heading towards Salir on a road that was even more tortuous as it wound down into the valley bottom.

'So where are we going?' he asked at last.

'Pena – near Pena.'

He pictured the map in his mind's eye. Pena. Maybe twenty miles. Not far for the crow, but in this hill country another world.

'What have you got in mind?'

'There is a small house there that once was a farm, but now is not. The people, they moved away. Abandoned it.'

'So it's empty now, unoccupied?'

'Not all the time. Someone goes there occasionally.'

'Do we need a key?'

'I know where there is a key.'

He nodded and felt relieved. It sounded like somewhere they could stop, rest and take stock, which they badly needed to do. The speed of events back there had almost overwhelmed him.

Chapter 15

The road became increasingly narrow, and ever more twisty. Past Salir they turned onto an even smaller road that took them to Alcaria. There, they took a single track road leading to Rocha da Pena, and after several slow miles they approached a small cluster of buildings straddling the road.

'Where now?' Jake asked, slowing down almost to a halt. He hadn't a clue where they were. This was all new to him.

'Just a little further.' Magda leant forward and peered intently through the dust-covered windscreen, and the darkness beyond. 'Where the little café is, turn to the right.'

He did, and their headlights showed a narrow and rising rough track that could only have been made by something like a bulldozer.

'Up here?' he asked, peering ahead uncertainly.

'A little way, yes.'

In first and second gear, they jolted and bumped their way a couple of hundred yards up the steep track, spewing a fan of loose stones and clouds of dust behind them. Jake was thankful they had all-wheel drive. The Honda was equal to the task, but he doubted his old truck would have made it.

'Here!' Magda pointed to their left.

He slowed almost to a stop and turned the car through a narrow gap in a wall of dense vegetation. They slowly climbed an even steeper track that led after a short distance up to a small, single-storey house surrounded by palms and olive trees.

'We are here,' Magda announced with satisfaction.

'Good thing it's painted white.' Jake chuckled. 'We would never have seen it otherwise.'

He drew to a halt, pulled on the parking brake and switched off the engine. He left the lights on for a few more moments while he studied the house. Then he turned them off and opened the door to get out.

'Let's take a look.'

'I will get the key,' Magda said, heading for the small terrace outside the front door of the house.

Jake watched her disappear into the shadows. Briefly, he wondered how she knew this place, and how she knew where there was a key. Yet another little mystery, he thought with a smile. Magda was full of them.

His eyes wandered over what he could see of the house. It looked to be a typical small, rural dwelling, a simple, traditional farmhouse essentially. He thought that until not so very long ago – before Portugal entered the EU, say, in the mid eighties – a family would have lived here on what they could produce from their own little patch of land: olives, carobs, pine nuts, vegetables, chickens, and a pig or two each year.

All that would have been supplemented by earnings from occasional, seasonal or part-time work elsewhere. A typical Algarve hill farm, then. Providing hard work and a hard life, without many luxuries, but in its way a good, steady life, and a safe one. A lot of people around the world would still settle happily for that, if they could have it.

Like a lot of others in the Algarve, though, this family farm had long been abandoned. The livestock were gone, the fruit trees left un-pruned, and the vegetable garden was overgrown and returned to wilderness. Entry into the EU, and the global market economy, had been the catalyst for change. That, and tourism. There were easier ways now to make a better living, and the old ways never had suited everyone anyway.

He moved behind the car to the edge of the drive to gaze down the hillside into the darkness of the valley below. Not a light to be seen down there. But on the opposite hillside, a couple of miles away, there were several clusters of lights: the village of Pena, and smaller places strung along the main road.

It looked fine to him. This was good, lonely country. They would be OK here. For a time. Until he had worked out what to do.

'I have the key,' Magda called softly.

He turned to join her as she opened the front door.

Inside, too, it was a simple cottage, a little white-washed stone box of a building, with window and door frames that had once been proudly painted the traditional blue but now were mostly flaked and bare. There was the room where a family had once lived, cooked and ate, and there was the bedroom. Water was drawn from the pump outside the back door. The white sink in the kitchen area was as close as the cottage got to having a bathroom. A smelly earth closet in the back garden, Jake guessed, would be the other principal facility.

Magda struck a match she took from a box on the kitchen table. That enabled them to locate a couple of candles. Jake lit one, and with the aid of that found an oil lamp. The lamp looked new, and thankfully had oil in it.

'That's better,' he said with a smile when the wick caught alight.

'The house is not much,' Magda said apologetically. She glanced around and shrugged.

'It's fine,' Jake assured her. 'Perfect. We won't be here long anyway.'

'No?'

He shook his head. 'All we needed was somewhere safe, while we work out what we're going to do.'

'Yes,' she said dubiously. 'Now I will heat some water for coffee.'

'With what?'

'There is a camping gas stove and kettle, and also tins and jars of food.'

He nodded, wondered again how she knew so much about the cottage, and let her get on with it. He was grateful. Who the cottage belonged to was a question that occupied him only briefly. It was too far down his list of priorities to detain him for long.

Even their more pressing problems didn't really engage him. He simply felt enormously relieved and thankful that they had been able to get out of São Brás in one piece and find a place of refuge. The way he felt just then, nothing else really mattered.

Chapter 16

They sat down around the well-worn pine table in the kitchen area, in a pool of soft yellow light from the oil lamp, mugs of coffee before them. It should have been quiet, but it wasn't.

Jake could hear night creatures outside, all around the house. An owl hunting, the buzz of insects, and something bigger snuffling and snorting. Wild boar or porcupine, perhaps? Even the house itself was making noises, as it recovered from the heat of the day and settled down for the night.

Not at all quiet, then. More comfortably noisy. Plenty of sounds to let them know they were not alone, but also that they wouldn't be troubled. Jake began to relax.

'I owe you an explanation,' he said softly.

Magda shrugged. 'We have our own histories, if that's what you mean. You will tell me what you want me to know when you are ready – if you want to, that is.'

He smiled with appreciation. He couldn't have put it better himself. She had a way with words, even in a language not her own.

'I will tell you now. Some of it, at least. It's time, past time. I had no right to bring all this down on you. I never intended it, either.'

'I am your woman,' she said, as if that explained and accounted for everything.

He started talking then, telling her how it had been for the past couple of years, and where and when it had all started.

He told her about Bob, and the warning he had delivered, and how swiftly the forces arraigned against him had moved and got their pieces in position on the board. It took quite some time. He even told her of things he had almost forgotten himself. In the telling, he found some relief, and a degree of hope for the future. This was his story. The telling of it made it feel as if he was back in charge, in control.

Magda listened patiently, calmly. She nodded occasionally but didn't interrupt him. Her questions and comments waited until he had finished, and even then there were not many.

'So you are not alone in this? Others, too, are threatened?'

He nodded. 'There are five of us now, that I know about. There used to be more. But the woman, Anna, has been murdered.'

'Five, now?' Magda said slowly, frowning, as if she had some doubts about the number.

'Unless you know otherwise?' he said with a smile.

'Me, Jake? How could I...?'

'Joke, Magda. It was a joke.'

Jesus, he thought. She takes everything so seriously. For a moment there she had seemed ready to launch an attack on him.

'Such a lot of money missing, Jake,' she said now, wonderingly. 'Twenty million pounds, in sterling?'

'So Bob told me,' he said with a shrug.

'Do you have it, Jake? Did you come to Portugal with it?'

'What do you think?' he said with a smile.

'I think maybe you don't have it,' she said with a coy smile of her own.

'And you're right.' He shook his head and sighed. 'I have no idea what happened to it. I didn't even know it was missing until Bob told me.'

'But you drove the van containing the money?'

'Some of it. Yes, I drove a van, but I didn't say it was the only one. There were two. That much cash, in banknotes, takes up a hell of a lot of space. Besides, Fogarty wouldn't have wanted all his eggs in one basket. He's too canny for that.'

'I understand. So one of the others drove another van?'

'Somebody did.' He frowned. 'I have no idea who, though. I just did my bit, what I was told to do. There was so much going on that night, and so much chaos, I didn't know what was happening to anybody else. I didn't know what everyone else was supposed to do, anyway. I was just a lowly emergency driver brought in at the last minute.'

'But now this man – Fogarty? – has come here to the Algarve, looking for you to kill?'

'Nicely put! Him, or men sent by him.'

'But why you? You say you were not important. It wasn't your fault it all went wrong.'

'That's true. But I was one of the people who betrayed him, and who spoke against him from the witness box. We're all on his hit list.'

He shrugged and added, 'Then there's the money. He'll be looking for that, as well.'

After a moment, Magda said, 'They wouldn't want just to kill you, I think.'

He shook his head, but he didn't say anything more. He didn't need to. It sounded as if Magda had already worked out the rest. Death would be a welcome relief from the questioning Fogarty would initiate, if it came to that. Preventing the questioning ever getting started was the challenge he faced.

He frowned as he thought about a word he had used earlier. Betrayal. That's what had happened that night in the Team Valley. Fogarty would want revenge against all those who had betrayed him, in whatever way. Nicci, especially. But all the others, too, himself included.

Some, he didn't even know about. But Fogarty would be intent on finding them all, even those that had disappeared back to far-flung places like Glasgow and Moscow. Maybe even Chicago or Los Angeles. Fogarty wouldn't rest until he had found them all, or was stopped in his tracks.

He yawned. He was tired now.

'Fogarty will believe that at least one of us knows what happened to the money. So he'll track us down, one by one, until he finds it. His questions won't be asked gently, either.'

'And will they always end with a bullet in the head?'

'Yes,' he admitted, surprised by her pragmatic, knowing question. 'Always. If his victims are lucky, that is. It could be worse.'

She thought about that for a moment and then said, 'So we must work out what to do.'

'We?' He gave a weary smile. 'This is my problem, Magda, not yours.'

'Now it is mine, too.'

'Yes, I suppose you're right,' he admitted, on reflection. Then he added, 'Come on! That's more than enough for one day. Let's try to get some sleep.'

'One more question, Jake. Before you became a van driver for this ... this bank robber, what were you? How did you live?'

'You wouldn't believe me if I told you.'

She waited patiently, staring at him

He shrugged. 'I was a retired spy. OK?'

'I thought it must have been something like that,' she said.

Chapter 17

The only bed in the cottage was a simple timber base with a thin foam mattress on top, behind a curtain at one end of the room. It looked clean enough. There was bedding in a cupboard, but they left it there. It smelled as if it had been there a long time. They didn't need it, anyway. The night was very warm.

They laid down together and Magda was soon asleep. Jake envied her. He couldn't make it. Too much had been happening. The adrenaline was still pumping. It was as much as he could do just to lie down.

He spent the hours of darkness on edge, restless, dozing but listening, waiting for the door to crash open and Fogarty to appear. It wasn't rational; it was survival instinct. The old fight-or-flight state of readiness that most creatures on the hillside around them would also be in that night, and most nights of their lives. Only predators could be relaxed, unless they were very hungry.

Reflecting, he was surprised that Magda had come with him so unquestioningly. Surprised, but grateful. In advance, he had tried to get rid of her, to clear the decks, in order to be unencumbered. In the old days he had always worked alone, and it was how he had preferred to be. Responsible for no-one but himself. But the old days were long gone, and he was glad to have Magda here with him. Lucky, too, he thought with a wry smile. Without her, where would he have gone when he fled São Brás?

Briefly, he wondered again how she had known about the cottage, and who it was that owned it. Obviously, she had been here before, perhaps a number of times. He shrugged. He didn't want to think about all that. He didn't want to start speculating about Magda's past life, either. He had enough in the here and now to think about, and to worry about.

When the suggestion of first light began to filter around the edges of the shutters on the windows, he gently eased away from Magda and slipped off the bed. He picked up his shoes and crossed the room to the door. Carefully, he eased the bolt aside and silently lifted the sneck on the door handle. Then he opened the door and slipped outside to take stock.

Four in the morning, and a beautiful morning at that. Not a hint of wind. The air fresh, and cooler now than it would be at any time in the day ahead. The sun would be up over the horizon in a little while, and would soon disperse the thin, patchy mist that had gathered overnight below in the valley. He glanced up at a clear sky that would turn blue with the coming of the day.

Behind him, towering over the cottage, was the great mass of Rocha da Pena, a mile-long, limestone hill rising to a height of 1,500 feet. In the early light the rugged buttresses and walls, bare of vegetation, were austere and daunting. The jumble of boulders and shattered trees and tough scrub covering the slopes beneath were no doubt home to a myriad species of wildlife, but they looked as inhospitable as anything he had seen in the Algarve. It was hard country.

Not a bird or animal of any description in sight, not that that was everything. There never were many birds to be seen, for reasons that eluded him, but there would be plenty of animals out looking for breakfast. Too cool for the likes of snakes yet, but there would be lynx and smaller raptors, such as mongoose, as well as all those creatures happy with a vegetarian diet. The land would abound in wildlife, however spartan it looked. Its warmth guaranteed that.

And now there was Fogarty to add to the list of raptors. No sign of him here yet, thankfully. No sign of anybody. No visible sign, at least, but he caught a whiff of wood smoke from somewhere. So somebody must live not far away. Another small farm, presumably, one that hadn't been abandoned. The wife up early to light the wood stove by which she cooked and heated water.

He glanced up at the luxuriant wisteria threatening to bring down the pergola that provided shade for the terrace. Dry country on the surface, but somehow plants like the wisteria found the water they needed down deep. Good growing country, really. It supported wisteria, cistus and all the other flowering plants and shrubs, together with the bushes and trees that produced the nuts and fruit that had made the Algarve a favoured agricultural region even in ancient times.

This little farm, he reflected, must have been just about self-sufficient. Now it was light, he could see the cork oak and the eucalyptus, and the trees that had produced the olives and almonds, and the lemons and oranges. A little distance from the house were the sheds and coops that had housed the livestock that provided the meat. What more could have been needed?

When he looked at it, he could see that the house itself had been built from the materials that lay and grew all around here. Earth and rock for the walls, pebbles for the terrace, bamboo canes for the interior ceilings. Local materials would even have given them the materials they needed to make their own whitewash and the blue paint used traditionally for the adornment of doorways and window frames.

No doubt about it. This little farm would have given a family a good life, up until the time when they had found a way of doing even better for themselves elsewhere. He smiled ruefully. It was hard not to feel sentimental about what had been lost.

He didn't hear Magda's approach, and he started as her arms slipped around him.

'Nervous?' she asked with a coy smile.

'You shouldn't do that,' he told her gruffly.

'Pff!' she said, hugging him hard.

He turned and wrapped his arms around her in return, but he was not pleased. He was unhappy, annoyed with himself. He hadn't heard her coming. That was very worrying, troubling. He needed to do better. He needed to be more alert. There was no such thing any more as safety and security, not unless he earned it.

Jake felt a need to explore their surroundings. So after a makeshift breakfast of figs from a nearby tree and stale crackers from a tin in a cupboard, accompanied by coffee, they stepped outside to venture further afield. They set off to walk up the track that climbed the hillside.

'I could smell wood smoke when I first came outside,' he said.

'From a bush fire?'

He shook his head. 'From a stove, I think. Someone must live around here.'

'I don't know,' Magda said, shrugging. 'Maybe.'

'We need to know,' he said firmly.

Just after eight now. And already it was hot, hot and dry. Later, Jake thought, it would probably get really hot. Maybe as much as forty degrees in the shade. They were in the fierce interior of the Algarve, some distance from the cooling influence of the ocean.

A strange looking figure suddenly came into view, rounding a bend in the track ahead of them just when they had become accustomed to the idea that they were alone. The figure was walking downhill towards them, moving with short strides and oddly precise footsteps. Something about the head, or where the head should be, was odd, too. Magda clutched his arm.

'It's all right,' Jake said quietly. 'Nothing to worry about.'

'Are you sure?'

By then, he was. The figure had become a woman, an elderly woman wearing something like a black top hat above a black jacket and a long, dark skirt that reached to her ankles. No wonder her movement had seemed strange, he realized as she drew nearer. She was wearing polished shoes with heels, low heels admittedly, but still shoes that would have been more appropriate on city pavements. The rough track was a struggle for her.

'Bom dia!' Good day, he said with a polite smile as they passed.

'Bom dia,' the woman responded, stony-faced.

Her eyes swept across him to Magda, where they lingered for a moment, until Magda, too, muttered a greeting.

Then she was gone. They continued on their way, Jake managing to resist the temptation to look back after her. Not for one moment did he think she would be looking back at them, but she had seen, definitely noticed, them both. That was unfortunate.

'Who is she?' Magda whispered.

Jake shook his head. 'No idea. But it doesn't matter,' he insisted, hoping that was true.

Already, though, he was thinking that perhaps they shouldn't stay here. They had been noticed, and they didn't fit. In places like this, unexplained strangers could be a worry, and a subject for gossip.

Magda's question was answered a couple of hundred yards further up the track, where they passed a small house hidden amongst low trees and scrub. An elderly man was chopping firewood for the stove. He looked up as they passed. Jake raised a hand in salute, and the man nodded back.

'So she was going to do her marketing,' Magda said thoughtfully.

Jake nodded. 'Catching a bus to town, probably. Properly dressed and shod for the occasion. The highlight of her week.'

'Shod?'

'Her shoes.'

'Ah! Which town, though?' Magda asked. 'And who will she see there?'

They were questions that worried him, too. The woman had seen them. Who would she tell?

Chapter 18

While they were walking, Jake recalled puzzling over something during the night, while he dozed and almost, but not quite, went to sleep. Something to do with Bob. Something he had said, or not said. Something about him. Some question. Odd. What the hell was it?

Bob was back in mind now. He could see him, but the picture was murky, cloudy. Something strange about it. But he was damned if he could put his finger on it.

'That's far enough for me,' Magda said, suddenly stopping walking. 'I want to go back to the house now.'

'Yes, of course.' He smiled and came to a halt beside her. 'We've seen enough. Let's go back, and sort out what we're going to do next.'

With surprise, he noted that he was beginning to include Magda in his thinking and planning automatically now. Well, why not? She was aboard, alongside him, regardless of whether or not that had been his original expectation.

Then his mind jumped to something else: a picture of Bob in uniform. He realized that was what he had been puzzling over in the night – a picture out of focus, but definitely of Bob in uniform. Why? What was the significance of that? Ridiculous! He smiled and shook his head. Whatever next? The pressure, the tension, was getting to him.

And then, in a eureka moment, it occurred to him that perhaps it wasn't ridiculous at all. There was a good reason for his preoccupation with Bob. It concerned an outstanding question. He needed to find the answer to that before they went much further.

Back on the terrace outside the cottage, he checked and found to his surprise that he had mobile coverage. Perhaps it shouldn't have been a surprise. Countries like Portugal, with poor landline infrastructure, had invested heavily in facilities for mobile services. It had been a cheaper option, and far speedier, than upgrading ancient landline networks.

Magda looked at him quizzically.

He made an apologetic gesture. 'I want to make a phone call.'

She shrugged and went inside, leaving him on the terrace. He made the call.

'Good morning. I would like to speak to DCI Robson.'

'May I ask your name, sir?'

'Just tell him it's Jake.'

After a pause a new voice came on the line. 'DCI Pendergast here. How can I help?'

'I want to speak to DCI Robson, if you don't mind.'

'I'm sorry. He's not available. Perhaps you can tell me what it's about? I'm sure I can help.'

Jake grimaced, ended the call and switched off the phone.

Magda, who had emerged with mugs of coffee, glanced at him curiously but didn't say anything.

'Bob,' Jake said. 'I wanted to speak to him, but he's not there.'

'The policeman? Perhaps it would be better if he doesn't know where you are.'

'Mm. Perhaps.'

He wondered about that. Shrewd Magda had a point. On the other hand, there was something he really did need to know. He'd better ask someone else. A possibility came to mind.

'There's another call I want to make.'

'If you must, Jake. But it is risky, I think.'

He was surprised by her comment, but knew she was right.

Most of all, though, he was surprised that Magda thought like that.

He phoned a man in a village in Northumberland, back in England, a man who had been the police sergeant there until he retired.

'Morning, Ken! This is Jake Ord. Remember me?'

'Jake? I just about remember you. How are you doing, lad? Haven't seen you for a long time.'

'I'm fine, thanks, Ken. Retirement suiting you?'

'Like a slipper! I can recommend the easy life.'

'That's good to know. Listen, I want to get in touch with DCI Bob Robson. You wouldn't have a personal phone number for him, would you? I know you were friendly with him, and I don't want to go through the switchboard and official channels.'

'Bob Robson? Oh, yes. We're old pals, and we see each other from time to time. He's in the same situation as me now, you know. We're both men of leisure.'

'So Bob's retired, as well, is he?'

'He has been for a few months.'

'Well, well. I didn't know that.'

He waited patiently and thanked Ken when he gave him a phone number for Bob.

'That's his private number, by the way. Nothing to do with the police.'

'I understand.'

'When are you going to fix that cottage up, Jake? Still planning on doing it?'

'Sometime, Ken. Yes, I'll be back one day, when I've got some money together.'

'Be sure to drop in. I'll maybe give you a hand.'

'Thanks, Ken. I'll remember that.'

'Cottage?' Magda said.

'You heard that, did you?' He smiled ruefully. 'Used to be a cottage. It got burned down.'

'In England?'

'In England, yes. Northumberland, actually. Know where that is?'

Magda shook her head.

'Northern England, close to the Scottish border.'

'I always wanted to visit England,' she said with a wry smile.

'No reason why you shouldn't,' he told her. 'One day, perhaps.'

'Yes.' She nodded. 'One day.'

The phone call had left him wondering. Retired, eh. So what was Bob's game? There had been a lot to think about already. Now he had something more to think about.

Chapter 19

The phone rang for a while before it was answered.

'Yes?'

'Morning, Bob! So you made it back home all right?'

There was a pause. Then: 'Jake?'

'It is.'

'I didn't recognize the number, bonnie lad.'

'No? Never mind. You got back all right. That's the main thing.'

'No problem. What's up? What are you doing, calling me?'

'You didn't tell me you were retired, Bob.'

Another pause. Jake gave a wry smile. He'd struck a nerve.

'Didn't I?' Bob said with a sigh. 'Well, we hadn't been in touch for a while. I was forgetting. But there it is. Doesn't make any difference, does it?'

'I'm not sure.'

He allowed a pause of his own to develop then. Bob needed to know he wasn't impressed.

'So you're working on your own now? Working for yourself? Is that it?'

'Trying to look after some good people, Jake, people I don't want coming to harm. People like you.'

Jake let that comment fade before he responded. Maybe it was true; maybe it wasn't.

'So who knows you're doing this, Bob? Anyone? Anyone at all?'

The other man chuckled. 'Worried about leaks still? Let

me tell you...'

'No, Bob. Just curious. You said there's a lot of money still missing from the heist.'

'What about it?'

The tone almost aggrieved now. Resentful.

'How much did you say again?'

'Oh, I don't know now!'

'Twenty million, wasn't it?'

'Roughly.'

'Sterling. Used banknotes.'

'Yeah.'

'Now we're getting to it,' Jake said. 'So, Bob, is it really the former colleagues you're interested in, or is it the cash?'

'Find the one,' Bob said equably, 'and you'll find the other.' He gave a little laugh. 'That what this call is about?'

'What do you think? There'll be a lot of people interested in money like that, Bob. Not just Fogarty, either. Have you been retained by someone to find the missing millions?'

'Well... Not exactly.'

'Not exactly, eh? But you do have an interest?'

'All kinds of interest, Jake. What do you want me to say, for chrissake?'

Jake gave a grim chuckle. 'Nothing, Bob. There's no need for you to say anything more to me again – ever!'

'Where are you calling from, Jake?'

Jake switched off the phone. He looked around, and saw Magda staring at him.

'I've always thought he was a friend,' he said bleakly. 'Now I need to think again.'

He walked up and down. To say he was irritated, or annoyed – angry even – would have been a significant understatement. He was blazing mad.

Bloody Bob! Stringing him along like that. All that crap about looking after decent people in terrible danger. And look what it amounted to! A retired cop looking to feather his nest. That was about it.

Involving him in the process, too. Wanting him to do the heavy lifting. Well, fuck that – and fuck him!

He walked off, and trudged back up the track a little way. Then he left it and took to a faint path climbing diagonally across the hillside. It was hot now. The morning was heating up as the sun got into its daily climb. He could feel the heat and the dust rising from the ground with every step he took. His feet crunched on the gritty soil, and pebbles splayed behind him. He followed the suggestion of a path that had probably been made by animals of some sort, as it meandered between boulders that had crashed down from the craggy escarpment above.

Insect noise all around him. The clicking and rasping of wings, the hissing and whirring of flight. All around him, amongst the rocks and the papery pink flowers of the cistus that clung so stubbornly to the hillside.

The path swung round eventually and steered straight uphill, perhaps as the animals that had made it turned for their homes on the upper slopes and the plateau of Rocha da Pena at the end of a night's hunting. They would return at night to their hunting ground, down here.

He became tired suddenly, breathless, soaking with sweat and exhausted. This was hard work, and it wasn't what he had set out to do. He wasn't in shape for hill climbing. Twenty minutes, and he'd had enough. He flopped down beside a big rock and wiped his face with the sleeve of his shirt. The sweat was pouring off him. And his legs ached, threatening to cramp. He knew he'd come too far. He wasn't up to this.

Better get in shape, he told himself. If you're going to take this any further, you need to rebuild. No more lazing around in the shade with a bottle of cheap wine. Got to take it seriously. Because Fogarty will. It won't be just an ordinary game for him. He's playing for high stakes, and he'll go all out.

Then: Bloody Bob! he thought bitterly. What a letdown. The end of what had seemed a beautiful friendship – and for what? A few quid! That was all it had taken. No sooner thought than a reluctant smile emerged. Who would have thought it? All it had taken was the lure of twenty million quid.

The smile became a grin. So Bob, the perfect cop, was human, after all? Mustn't be too hard on the guy, though. Hell, plenty of folk would sell their own mothers for twenty million quid!

Bob wouldn't be expecting that much, of course. Not the whole twenty million. He was probably working with an insurance company, on some sort of commission basis. He would be looking for a percentage of however much he managed to recover for them.

Now just hang on a minute! Bob? Bob wasn't going to find anything for them. He was wanting someone else to do that for him, while he sits safely and comfortably at home.

That thought made him want to spit. So he did. It gave him the chance to get rid of some of the grit in his mouth, as well as the bile.

The rattle of pebbles sliding down the hillside brought his head swinging round, his pulse racing. He could see nothing. But the sound had come from behind him, along the path he had followed. He waited, tense, listening.

Another minute flew by. He heard nothing more. Nothing happened. Something was out there, but what?

A head appeared, shimmering in the heat waves lifting from the scree. He stared hard until the wavy lines stilled. Then he relaxed.

'Worried about me?' he called.

'A little,' Magda admitted. 'You've been gone a long time.'

'Sorry.'

'You shouldn't have gone without me.'

'I needed to think.'

He waited and watched her draw close, moving easily at a steady pace. She seemed pretty fit, more so than he had realized. Just natural, he supposed. Natural fitness. Some people had it. Not like him. He had always had to work at it.

'So did you do that?' she asked as she reached him. 'Think?'

'Some. I'm getting my head straightened out a bit.'

'About your friend Bob?'

He nodded.

'Maybe he is your friend still – or could be again?'

He shook his head and sighed. Then he stared at her, wondering if she was thinking the same way he was.

'It is a lot of money,' she pointed out. 'Too much for one person.'

He chuckled. 'Too much for Bob, anyway, even if he only gets half of it.'

'Does he want all of it?'

Jake shook his head. 'I doubt it. He wouldn't know what to do with that much money. I think he must be working for an insurance company. He'll be looking to get a percentage of whatever he recovers.'

'So anything he gets would be legal?'

'That's right. Not stolen money. Reward. Clean money.'

Magda nodded, and said nothing more for a while. She lowered herself onto a rock beside him. They sat together in silence, gazing unseeingly at the landscape spread out below them, working through the implications. It didn't take long for them to get there.

'With even some of the money...' Magda began.

'Yeah. You're right. We could do things. Rebuild my cottage, for a start.'

'In England? It is my dream to go to England,' she said with a smile.

He wondered if it was a mistake to have spoken aloud, and included her in his thinking. Well, why not? They had been together for a while, and she was here still. Right now, when he needed someone, she was here. They were partners.

Partners? He realized that was the idea he had been unconsciously exploring. He needed to be pragmatic, realistic.

Suddenly, the way ahead seemed clear and straightforward now.

'I'll offer Bob a deal, a partnership,' he said briskly.

'I think that would be wise,' Magda said, as if she had been thinking the exact same thing.

Chapter 20

He called Bob again.

'Yes, Jake?' Bob said warily.

'I take it you're working with an insurance company?'

'What's wrong with that?'

'Nothing. It's not what I understood, that's all. You didn't tell me. So things are different now. You're no longer a serving police officer, for one. That's important – to me, at least.'

Magda was keeping out of the way, letting him get on with it, but even though he couldn't see her, he knew she was hanging on his every word. She wanted him to get this right, bless her!

'That's how it is, Jake. What do you want me to say?'

Sorry, Jake thought between gritted teeth. That would do for a start. Well, at least he knew where he stood. Theirs could only be a business relationship from now on.

'I want in, Bob. A partnership. Fifty-fifty – and no more bullshit about how your only interest is in trying to help former colleagues and save innocent lives.'

Bob chuckled. 'The two of us working together, eh? That's what you want?'

'That's my price for doing the dirty work and taking the risks, out in the field, Bob. You can stay right where you are. Use your contacts, gather the information, keep things in order. I don't want you actually with me.'

'I have no problem with that, bonnie lad. I'm a bit long in the tooth anyway for fieldwork.'

Bob more like his old self now, remembering who he was. Who he used to be, at least. The authority and quiet confidence back in his voice. Just remember not to trust him again, Jake thought. His true colours had been revealed.

'In fact, Jake, I hoped it would come to this. You and me, working together again.'

Oh, aye? Really?

'So what's the arrangement with the insurance company?'

'I – we, that is, now – get twenty per cent of whatever we recover. That's what I negotiated. Now don't you go thinking that's four million quid in our pocket! It could be, theoretically, but we may not get anything at all, and we certainly won't get the full whack. We haven't a cat in hell's chance of finding the whole twenty million, not after all this time.'

'Fair enough. I hear what you say.'

'So you're in?'

'Yeah.'

'What's your current location?'

'I'm not far from where I was when I saw you last. When I arrived home from that meeting, they were waiting for me. I had to get out fast.'

'Fogarty's people?'

'Who else? I didn't actually make their acquaintance, but I'm sure it was them all right.'

'But you gave them the slip?'

'Somehow.'

'Good for you.' Bob paused, thinking it through. 'Take your time, bonnie lad. And keep out of trouble – as much as you can. Make a start, and let me know how you get on.'

'I'll do that.'

'One more thing, Jake. Be careful. Don't trip over Fogarty by accident. He's dangerous. He'll bite.'

'Point taken.'

Jake switched off and shook his head.

'It was OK?' Magda asked.

'I think so. Our troubles may be only just starting, but I've got an agreement with Bob that ought to stick.'

'Good.'

She didn't seem to want to know more. Just as well, Jake thought. He had little more to tell her.

Sitting on the terrace outside the cottage that afternoon, they saw their elderly neighbour returning from her outing. Her shopping basket had things in it now. She switched it from one hand to the other, coping with the weight. Walking uphill now, she needed to pause to rest from time to time.

Jake went out and offered to help with her shopping, but she shook her head and mumbled a word of thanks. He raised his eyebrows in polite enquiry to see if she was sure. She smiled and started walking again.

'She's too old to be living up here,' Jake remarked when he rejoined Magda. 'And her husband looked even older.'

'It's what they do, old people,' Magda said with a sigh. 'Be independent and keep going as long as they can. I used to see it in my village. Here, there may be no alternative anyway. No possibility of help. So they live as best they can, and then they die.'

He nodded. 'You're probably right.'

'It is best not to get old.'

He chuckled. 'If Fogarty catches up with us, getting old won't be an option we'll have!'

Chapter 21

Jake woke with a start and glanced at his watch. Two a.m. Something must have disturbed him. Instantly wide awake, he lay still, listening, concentrating. Beside him, Magda was sleeping soundly, breathing steadily, her face turned towards him. But he knew something had woken him.

He slipped off the bed and across to the front window. The night was dark. No cloud, but no moon, either. Starlight only out there. He could see next to nothing. He turned to collect the Glock pistol. Then he eased the door open quietly and stepped outside.

Listening still. Hearing nothing, at first. Then he heard the unmistakable crunch of boots on gravel, and the rattle of stones inadvertently dislodged and knocked aside.

Someone was coming up the track. More than one person, he realized, as he heard a stumble followed by a whispered exchange. Time to go, he thought, heart beating fast.

'What is it?' Magda whispered as he stepped back inside.

'People are coming,' he said, reaching for his boots. 'I'll try to stall them. Grab our stuff, and get out the back way. But keep away from the car.'

There was no time for more. He heard Magda scrambling in the dark, and left her to it. They had agreed to be prepared to leave at a moment's notice, and there was nothing to pack anyway. They just had to get out.

He went back outside, stepped down from the terrace and made his way to the entrance to the short drive.

'What do you want?' he called, in English, before moving quickly to a new position under the trees.

A powerful torch swept over the place where he'd been standing. He closed his eyes for a moment to avoid losing his night vision.

'That you, Ord?'

There was even less doubt about who they were now. He didn't bother wondering how they had found him so fast. They were here. That was all that mattered.

Three or four of them, he guessed, as he heard feet leave the track and bodies crash through the undergrowth. There was more calling and questioning, but he didn't wait and he didn't answer. He slipped away through the olive grove and moved fast to the nearest corner of the cottage.

Magda was waiting there. He grabbed her arm and turned to hustle her away through the trees and shrubs, heading uphill. Once again, he was thankful she didn't argue or want to discuss things first. There was no time for that. No time for anything, in fact.

Past the last of the olive trees, the going became much more difficult. They ran into a tangle of dense undergrowth, maquis scrub with spikes and thorns. It was wild land, probably never cultivated, and further progress was next to impossible. Jake pressed hard for a minute or so, trying to ease the spikes and thorns aside, shielding Magda as best he could. Then he gave up, stopped and turned around.

'It's no good!' he whispered. 'We'd be better on the track.'

'Then let's try to reach it,' Magda said. She squeezed his arm for a moment, as if to encourage him.

Surprised, he nodded and turned to head across the slope towards the track, which wasn't far away. Unseen branches whipped at his face, and spines and prickles tore at his arms. He ignored them. They had to reach the track quickly, and then get well away from here if they were to avoid being spotted when first light arrived.

They made it sooner than he expected. Suddenly there was

nothing in front of him. Just space and cool air. He staggered awkwardly, rather than fell, down a short drop to the track. He turned to reach out a helping hand to Magda. She caught it, and managed to stay on her feet as she stumbled down to stand beside him.

'OK?' he whispered.

'I think so.'

Suddenly there was an explosion of light behind them. He swung round.

'It's the cottage!' he snapped. 'The bastards have torched it.'

'Oh, no!' In the new light he saw Magda's hand fly to her mouth.

'Come on!' he said. 'We can't stay here.'

They could see several figures milling about on the track a couple of hundred yards away, which probably meant they themselves would be visible, too. They turned and started off up the track, breaking into a run when shouts behind indicated they had been seen. It was a race now, against time as well as the men behind them.

He thought fast. A couple of hours to first light. Maybe less. Before then, they needed to find somewhere to hide.

Five minutes of hard running uphill had them both gasping for air and struggling to keep going. Jake was in no condition for this, and he didn't suppose Magda ever had been, fit as she was in a general sense.

What to do? The men coming after them were closing. The gap was only half what it had been, judging by what he could hear. They would have to get off the track soon, and just lie still. Hope for the best. Shoot it out if it came to that.

It didn't seem quite as dark as it had been. He could almost see a bend in the track coming up. He grabbed Magda's arm as they ran and hustled her along, hoping to God she didn't stumble and fall.

It was a bend, one with big trees either side. He could sense them, if not see them. His eyes began searching for a less dark patch in the blackness that might indicate a way off the track.

'Here!' a gruff whisper said suddenly out of the darkness. 'This way!'

Magda gasped with shock. Jake's head swung round. Automatically, he raised and pointed the Glock.

'This way,' the unseen speaker insisted. 'Quickly!'

Jake hesitated, but only for a moment. Then he stumbled to the side of the track, pulling Magda after him, heading for the source of the whispers.

Chapter 22

A hand grabbed Jake's arm and pulled him, and Magda with him, through the wall of vegetation alongside the track. An arm went around his back and pressed him forward. It felt like a man's arm, but in the confusion of the moment Jake could tell nothing else. He went with it.

Another hand, a gentler hand, reached out from somewhere in front to grasp him and pull him forward. He stumbled on, holding on to Magda, pulled blindly between the trees. A minute later, a whispering voice said they must stop and be absolutely quiet.

They stopped. Jake pulled an arm over his mouth and tried to muffle the harsh sound of his own breathing and panting. Seconds later, he heard boots pounding past on the track, and yelps and oaths as feet slipped and tripped over unseen obstacles. There were several men involved, one or two with wildly swinging torches.

They stood still for a minute or two more. Then an arm pressed them gently forward, and they began to move again, steering their way through scrub and trees. Whoever it was helping them seemed to be on familiar ground.

They didn't go far. When they stopped again, they were next to a high stone wall that gave off an old, earthy smell. Some sort of barn or animal shed. A door squeaked as it opened. Jake grimaced and held his breath, but a whispered instruction from behind urged him on into the blackness beyond. He heard the door shut behind them.

'One moment, please,' said a gruff male voice, low but no longer a whisper.

Jake stood still, holding Magda by the hand. He heard the sound of a match being struck. Light flared from it. He saw the figure of a man leaning over a work bench to light a small oil lamp. The darkness fled as the lamp gleamed into life. The man adjusted the wick, dimming the light a little.

'We haven't much time,' the man said, turning to them.

He was old and bent. He wore a plaid shirt and baggy trousers held up by a broad leather belt, and a flat cap made of leather. By then, Jake had realized who he was, and who the second person standing in the shadows behind them must be.

'You have the farm, higher up the track?' he asked.

The man nodded and pointed to the figure behind them. 'My wife, and I.'

Jake turned and smiled at the woman. He couldn't see her face but she raised a hand in acknowledgement.

'Thank you for helping us,' he said, turning back to her husband. 'But how did you know what was happening?'

'My wife heard men, strangers, plotting such a thing when she was doing her shopping in the town. We expected this, or something like this.' He shrugged. 'So we were waiting.'

He beckoned, and the elderly woman last seen coming home from market with a basket in hand stepped forward into the pool of dim light.

'You,' she said firmly, looking at Magda. 'I know you. You have been here before – with another man.'

'Yes,' Magda admitted. 'With my friend. He owns the house where we were staying. Thank you for helping us.'

The woman nodded, satisfied that her memory had not failed her.

'We are happy to help,' the man said, speaking quickly, 'but I think you must leave here very soon. Those men will come to our house, I think, to search for you. Soon it will be daylight. They will see this barn, and investigate.'

'Of course,' Jake said, nodding. 'You're right. We'll leave immediately.'

'I am sorry,' the man said, spreading his arms helplessly. 'But it will be for the best. We can't keep you safe.'

'No, no! Of course not. You must go home now, back to your house,' Jake said. 'They may well go there, but you have nothing to hide. You can show them that. You will be OK. They have no interest in you.'

'Let us hope,' the man said.

He set them on their way, steering them onto a little path they could follow.

'It will take you up to the top of the hill. Then you should make your way to Penina, the village below the far end of Rocha da Pena. The track those men are following will take them to the opposite end of the hill, perhaps three, four kilometres away. You will be a long way from them when morning comes. After that,' he added, 'I am afraid I do not know.'

'We will manage,' Jake assured him. 'Thank you,' he added gravely, shaking the man's hand. 'Thank you – and your wife. We are most grateful. One day—'

'Go now,' the man said, cutting him off, but not in an unkindly way. 'God be with you.'

As they set off along the path, Jake saw that in the night sky to the east he could see the first hint of the coming dawn. They were not a moment too soon.

'Are you all right?' he whispered over his shoulder to Magda.

'I think so.'

'Good. Let's press on then. We can talk later.'

The path was steep, and certainly not easy-going, but he could follow it without too much difficulty as it wound its way steadily uphill, through the thickets of spiny undergrowth and between the boulders and rocks. They had been incredibly lucky, he thought. Unbelievably so. But they were not out of it yet.

Best not to dwell on that, though. They had to get up the hill, and stay ahead of Fogarty's men. That had to be their focus now, and for the foreseeable future. One step at a time. They just had to get up this damned hill, and on to the nearby village.

Then what? He didn't know. Had no idea. And for the moment, at least, he didn't care.

It took them thirty minutes to complete the climb. He could hear Magda breathing heavily behind him but she never once complained or suggested resting. She kept up with him all the way.

Suddenly the slope eased off and they found themselves walking on level ground, following a path on red earth through thickets of scrub and low-growing trees. He could see animal tracks, hoof marks and paw prints, where the ground was soft. Hunters and the hunted, he thought grimly. Just like us. By then, the landscape was suffused with early morning light, grey, patchy, eerie.

'It is beautiful up here,' Magda said, breaking the silence that had enveloped them.

Jake glanced at her, and then around at their surroundings. 'Yes,' he said, 'I suppose it is. In other circumstances...'

She gave him a smile. They pressed on, heading for the western end of the plateau. Jake was looking to pick up the way down to the next village, which they could see now in the misty distance. Perhaps two or three miles to go, he thought. But then what?

'I think someone is coming,' Magda said, anxiously clutching his arm.

He paused, listening. Then he heard it, too. Dull thuds, the sound of several people moving fast, jogging. Very close. God, they'd been quick!

He glanced around desperately and pulled Magda into nearby bushes.

There wasn't any doubt at all about who they were. As soon as Jake saw the first of them, he was certain these was the same men who had fire-bombed the cottage. Four of them swept past at that ground-covering military pace that is too fast for walking but not quite running. A tough crew. Special forces trained, he guessed. Christ, they were up against something! These were not your ordinary Essex thugs.

After they had gone by and vanished into the mist and the scrubland, he said calmly, 'We can't outrun them, and we can't out-fight them. We may have made a mistake, coming up here.'

Magda nodded. 'Maybe.'

But she didn't sound too concerned about it.

'Are you thinking the same as me?' he asked with surprise.

'I don't know, Jake. What I'm thinking is that our car is still at the foot of the mountain. And even if it isn't, or if it has been set on fire, that's where theirs must be also.'

'You are thinking the same as me,' he said with a wry chuckle. 'Come on then! Let's go and see.'

Chapter 23

It was daylight now and they were going downhill, going down a lot faster than they had come up. Halfway down, Jake led the way off the path and steered a course that would take them close to the cottage that briefly had seemed such a safe refuge.

There was a lot on his mind. For a start, how the hell had Fogarty's people found them? So quickly, too. It was hard to believe. No-one had followed them when they fled São Brás. There had been no vehicle lights behind them at any point during their journey here. And they had told no-one where they were going. It didn't seem possible. But it had happened.

How then? All he could think was there must be some sort of tracker on the Honda. Shit! He hadn't thought of that. How likely was it? Not very, but he should have thought of that possibility and checked.

In fact, the more he thought about it, the more likely it seemed. What else was there?

He'd been too long retired, he thought with a grimace. He'd lost his instinct for survival. From now on, he was going to have to be a damned sight more careful.

But was a vehicle tracker the only possibility? Well, what else was there? Bob? Could he have let something slip?

He shook his head. Forget it. Bob had no idea where he was. All Bob knew was that he had been in São Brás, and Rocha da Pena was a long way from São Brás. Even further from Faro, not to mention Newcastle. It couldn't be anything to do with Bob.

'Jake?'

He managed to stop on the steep slope and spun round, his boots losing their grip on the stony surface, causing him to slide and slither a few feet.

'What?'

'Talk to me, Jake. You're leaving me out of your thoughts. I'm feeling like a passenger, a stranger.'

'Sorry. There's nothing to tell you.'

He wiped his face with one hand and glanced around anxiously. No sign of anyone else – yet!

'I was just wondering how they found us so fast,' he said.

'Me, too. It's not good.'

'Well, there's nothing we can do right now. Let's just focus on getting out of here in one piece.'

He turned to continue the descent. 'Ah! Is that our cottage I smell?'

It was, what was left of it. Down here, the air was full of acrid bonfire-like smoke, and the blackened heap they could see in the near distance was very much still smouldering. Not a cottage any more, actually, he thought. More a charred ruin. Four stunted, smoking walls without a roof or an interior.

It reminded him of another cottage, one in distant Northumberland. In another lifetime, that one had ended up like this.

'Not much left,' he observed. 'Your friend will be very disappointed when he next sees it.'

Magda shrugged. 'It is a pity,' was all she said.

Nothing more about her friend, Jake noted. But he didn't quiz her. It was her business, who she had been here with, and in what circumstances. The here and now was all that mattered. Magda wouldn't want to talk about previous relationships any more than he did himself.

It was curious, though, that the old woman had seen and remembered her on previous visits. What did that mean? Magda had been here often? Perhaps. Probably, in fact. She had known where a key was kept, after all.

Mysterious Magda, he thought with amusement. There was so much he didn't know about her. Well, she could say the same about him, couldn't she? Neither of them had been forthcoming about their pasts, their "personal histories", as Magda had put it. And now wasn't the time even to think of doing anything about it.

There seemed to be no-one around the ruined cottage, which wasn't surprising. There was nothing left to guard, or watch. Still...

Jake hesitated before making the final approach. He studied the scene. Where they stood, there was shelter. Rocks, trees, undergrowth. Any closer, coming from this side, and they would be out in the open. Vulnerable. Was there really no-one here?

'Can't see anyone,' he said quietly. 'Can't see the car, either.'

'No,' Magda agreed, 'and there is no smoke coming from where we left the car.'

'That's true.'

He studied the clump of trees next to the cottage. He couldn't see anything. No metal, and no smoke, either. Perhaps the Honda had been moved.

'Stay here,' he said. 'I'm going to see.'

Not waiting for Magda to say anything, he slipped away through the undergrowth, keeping low, moving fast.

There really was nobody around the burned-out cottage, he soon discovered. And the car really was there – and intact. So far as he could see, it was exactly as they had left it.

He got in and tried the ignition. All the lights came on. He turned the key further. The engine started first go. He nodded with satisfaction, and began to reverse out of the trees.

By the time he had reached the track and turned the car

round, Magda had arrived. 'The old man who helped us is there,' she said, pointing.

Jake got out and looked back up the track. The man was standing at the point where the track curved. Jake gave him a thumbs up, and the man waved farewell in return. It looked as though he was OK, which was a relief.

'Let's go!' he said, getting back in the car.

'They might have someone waiting with their vehicle at the bottom of the hill,' Magda pointed out.

Jake nodded. 'If they have, we'll deal with it.'

He set off slowly, and kept in a low gear all the way down. No point blowing out noise and dust clouds to anyone who might be waiting.

There was a double-cab, pickup truck at the bottom of the hill, parked sideways across the foot of the track, blocking it. One man had been left with the truck. He got out when he saw them coming, and stood in front of his vehicle. He held up a hand to stop them. With his other hand, he reached back inside the cab and came out with a shotgun.

When they were only fifteen or twenty yards away, Jake pressed his foot to the floor. The Honda took off. Too late, the man with the shotgun realized it wasn't going to stop. Feverishly, he raised and tried to steady the gun. Then his nerve failed. The arm holding the shotgun fell and he leapt sideways, desperate to get out of the way.

He was too late. The impact was softened by Jake taking his foot off the throttle and jamming it hard on the brake, but that didn't stop the scream.

Jake leapt out and grabbed the shotgun. Then he got back in and pulled the Honda back a yard or two. When he got out again, he was looking for information.

'My legs,' the man cried, in agony. 'You've bust my fucking legs!'

'Yeah? Too bad. Remind me – what were you going to do to us?'

'Nothing, nothing!'

'No, of course you weren't. Now, what I want to know is how you found us.'

'I don't know. Christ!' he whimpered, reaching towards his legs but not daring to touch them.

Magda broke in. 'I think they're coming, Jake!'

He looked round. She pointed along the road towards Penina. He saw she was right. A group of men moving fast were heading this way. No doubt they had seen or heard something.

It's a pity, he thought with a grimace. No time for more questions.

'Well,' he said, pulling out the Glock. 'I hope your mates are more sympathetic than me.'

'There's no need for that!' the man protested.

'Oh yes, there is!'

The man closed his eyes. Jake moved the gun aside and fired at the nearside front tyre. Then he quickly went around the vehicle, shooting out the other three tyres. The truck lurched as it settled on its rims.

He threw himself back in the Honda and got them moving. 'Nothing to say?' he asked, glancing sideways at Magda.

She shrugged. 'Now they can't follow us, I suppose.'

'That's right.'

'But I would have shot the man, as well.'

Jake chuckled. 'His mates might do that themselves! He's not going to be much use to them with two broken legs.'

'That is true.' She paused and then said, 'So where do we go now, Jake?'

'How about your country? It should be a damn sight safer than here.'

Chapter 24

Five miles down the road he pulled the car off onto a forestry track, drove a few yards until they were out of sight round a bend and then stopped. Magda looked at him.

'I want to check the car. See if someone has fixed a tracker on us.'

'Because they knew where we were, where to come for us?'

He nodded. 'Not knowing how they managed that is doing my bloody head in!'

He got out and took stock. He looked under the hood, and in the back of the vehicle. Then he ran his fingers along the undersides of the car, and still found nothing that shouldn't be there. He lay on his back, squirmed his way right under the car. Same thing. Nothing. Nothing he could see, anyway.

Shaking his head, he got back into the driver's seat. Then he drummed his fingers on the steering wheel and sat frowning, thinking about it.

'Doesn't mean there's nothing there, though,' he said at last, reaching for the ignition key.

They got going again. They drove back into São Brás, where Jake visited a little shop he knew that sold everything there was to do with computers, as well as gizmos for defeating speed traps. Stuff like that. Said what he wanted, and came away with a gadget that was said to be so powerful there wasn't a hope in hell of it not detecting something – if something was there.

The gadget found nothing.

'Right,' he said, a bit happier. 'It's not the car. They must have had some other way of keeping tabs on us.'

'Perhaps someone told them?'

He grimaced. He didn't even want to think about that possibility. There were only two people in the world he could think of who were in a position to be able to do anything like that: himself and Magda. Unless he had been talking in his sleep, and the fairies had recorded him doing it, it was unthinkable.

There was another possibility, though, a very obvious one once the car had been cleared of blame.

'It has to be our phones,' he said grimly. 'We'll dump them.'

He took out his phone and stripped out the sim card. Then he paused a moment, studying the body of the phone. 'This had better go, as well.'

He walked over to a big commercial rubbish container, lifted the lid and dropped the phone inside.

'Where's yours?' he asked Magda when he returned.

'I don't have it. It's in my apartment.'

'OK. Now let's go! Sadly, we must leave this little town, where until a day or two ago we were so very happy.'

'Yes indeed,' Magda said, wearing a solemn expression, as they got back in the Honda. 'Burn some rubber, Jake!' she added in a surprisingly good best gangster moll accent.

Jake looked at her with surprise. Then he laughed and got them moving again.

They sped up the EN2, up into the barrocal, and on into the caldeira, the mountains, beyond. They were headed for the Alentejo, and the wide open spaces of interior, rural Portugal, where life supposedly stood still. Jake hoped the guide books were right about that.

He drove all day and through the night after they left São Brás, and early the next morning they reached France. Nothing more had happened in the meantime. They had put a lot of miles behind them without any hint of a pursuit. He had gradually relaxed. Maybe they were in the clear now.

'You need to rest,' Magda suggested. 'Let me drive. You try to get some sleep in the back seat.'

He thought about it, and knew she was right. Magda didn't say an awful lot, but when she did speak he was starting to think it was worth listening.

'The next service area,' he said. 'I'll pull in, and we can swap over.'

She nodded. 'Sleep,' she said, 'and then we will talk some more about what has been happening.'

That, too, was a good suggestion. If she was to be with him, she needed to know more about where they stood and what they faced.

If she was to be with him? He still wasn't entirely sure about that. Maybe it would be better to get her home, to her own country, and leave her there. Safer for her, and less complicated for him.

It would make sense. After all, how could she be with him, given what he was contemplating? She really had no idea what she would be letting herself in for. Nor did he, come to that. Not really. All he knew was that he was going to be doing a lot of travelling, and probably experiencing a lot more of what they had been through in the past couple of days.

So. Give her up? Let her go?

He would think about it some more, he decided. No need to say anything right now.

They stopped and changed seats. Once he was satisfied that Magda knew how to handle the Honda, Jake settled on the back seat as best he could to try to snatch some sleep. Exhausted though he was, though, sleep didn't come easily, or quickly. As soon as he laid down and pulled a rug over his head to shut out the light, his mind went into overdrive. He retraced events since his return to the villa after meeting Bob in Faro. Then he did it all over again. He couldn't help it.

He knew he needed to get far away from all that, if only for a short time. He needed to recover, do some thinking and work out what he was going to do from now on. Where they were heading now was somewhere completely different, and hopefully might make that possible.

And Magda? Was that what she needed, too? Well, he thought wearily, Magda was pretty much an enigma. Who could say what she really thought and felt about anything – apart from him, seemingly. She had made that pretty clear. He was beginning to realize how little he knew about her otherwise, but that didn't stop him feeling glad she was with him – for now, at least.

He certainly wasn't going to complain about Magda being along for the ride. She had done well by him. There wasn't a single complaint he could make. It was just that he wasn't sure he wanted to encumber himself with responsibility for another human being. Nor did he want any harm to come to her, either.

He did finally drift off to sleep. When he woke up, Magda said they had done more than 500 kilometres while he slept. Now they were approaching Lyon. He sat up with a jolt.

'How are you doing?' he asked.

'I am fine, thank you. But you need to drive again, I think. And we need more diesel.'

He nodded. 'Pull in at the next service station. We'll get something to eat and drink while we're there.'

They bought baguettes and coffee, strong coffee, and sat in the little dining area with them, next to the shelves of chocolate bars and magazines.

The forecourt of the filling station was busy. Cars arriving and leaving every few seconds from the twenty or so pumps. The highway beyond was a constant stream of traffic. High-powered cars sweeping past in the fast lane, convoys of trucks in the slow lane, and the middle lane thronged with vans, saloons and coaches. Europe on the move, non-stop.

'What still puzzles me,' Jake said with a sigh, 'is how the hell they got on to us so fast. Was it through our phones? I certainly hope so, but if it was by some other means we'll still be at risk. However they did it,' he added, 'they certainly knew. They knew exactly.'

'Yes.' Magda nodded. 'The old lady told us that. She heard them talking in a café in the town.'

He sighed and shook his head. 'We'll just have to hope it was the phones that gave us away, but let's take nothing for granted. We'll have to stay vigilant, just in case.'

He knew they had been lucky, very lucky. They probably wouldn't have managed to escape without the help of the old couple.

'One day we must go back there, and thank them both properly,' he suggested.

'Perhaps.'

That didn't sound like much of a commitment, Jake thought with a little smile. So perhaps she wasn't so sentimental, after all. In a way, it was reassuring. They needed to focus on themselves, and the now, if they were to get away with this. Let the distant future look after itself.

'At least we are free of Fogarty for now,' he added.

'Perhaps,' Magda said again.

A realist, as well! He was glad of that, too.

'How long is it since you left home?' he asked with a yawn. 'When, and why, did you leave, for that matter?'

She chuckled. 'It would take all day to tell you, and we don't have the time. Perhaps we should go now?'

Practical, too, Jake thought, as he got up. I'm learning more about her every minute.

Magda's estimate of the travel time needed was spot on. It took three days to reach her country. They scarcely stopped on the way, Jake eager to put miles behind him, and intent on leaving no electronic trail as they went. They slept in the car, when they took time out to sleep, and he paid for the diesel and everything else they needed with cash.

The second day, they crossed France and Belgium, and drove a long way across Germany. Then they stopped for the night in a rest area on the autobahn near Chemnitz. The next morning, early, they by-passed Dresden and headed down to the valley of the Elbe.

'To us Czechs,' Magda said, 'it is the Labe, the River Labe. Elbe is the German name.'

'Is it? I didn't know that.'

'There is probably much that you don't know about my country,' Magda pointed out with a smile. 'Unless you did your spying there?'

He shook his head. 'No. All that was done in the Middle East – a long time ago.'

'Perhaps.'

That word again! He glanced at her and she laughed. He shook his head ruefully. She was just winding him up.

They followed the road along the riverside, passing between rows of picturesque timber cottages and going through several villages and small towns. Half an hour later, they crossed the border and entered the Czech Republic without any fuss at all. Schengen, Jake thought with relief. What a blessing the agreement was still in use, in this part of the continent at least.

With Magda directing him, he turned off the main road into a spectacularly picturesque Czech village nestling in a deep and incredibly narrow canyon. The road and a small river flowing through the canyon left little space for anything else, but somehow restaurants, hotels and shops had been carved out of and built into the sandstone walls.

'Hřensko. German tourists like it here,' Magda said with a disdainful sniff, as they passed market stalls selling shiploads of beer and shedloads of garden gnomes for those visitors with an itch to make their day out seem worthwhile.

'I'm not surprised,' Jake said, looking around with interest. Then he smiled. 'But you don't?'

She just shrugged.

They drove the length of the village and then climbed up into dense forest, the big trees coming to the very edge of the road on both sides of the narrow strip of tarmac.

'You would have to like trees – really like them a lot – to live here,' Jake pointed out after a few minutes.

'Oh, yes!' Magda said with chuckle. 'It is a fairytale forest, I think.'

They drove for another twenty minutes or so before they emerged into more open country. Still plenty of trees, but here there were open fields, too.

A few miles further on, as they approached a small huddle of buildings at the foot of a hill, Magda announced, 'We are here!'

'Oh?' Jake stared ahead with interest. 'Where's here?'

'Vysoká Lípa,' she said confidently.

Chapter 25

Vysoká Lípa was a hamlet with a name that literally meant "High Lime Tree", perhaps in recognition of the wonderful old tree in front of the ancient hotel, or perhaps not. It was a settlement, a wide scatter of houses, without a true centre, but the hotel itself was an adequate substitute. It stood on a bend at the highest point the road passing through Vysoká Lípa reached, overlooking everything else. Nearby was the bus stop and the tourist information panels, as well as boards with information for local residents.

A couple of dozen traditional timber houses straggled down the steep road from the hotel, and an equal number were set well back behind them. At the bottom of the hill were two restaurants, largely targeting German visitors from over the nearby border. Some of the houses in the village were guesthouses, or at least had rooms to let. Many others seemed to be weekend retreats, or holiday homes, for their owners.

'Do they get a lot of tourists here?' Jake asked.

Magda nodded. 'This area is called Czech Switzerland. So, yes, they do. Most of them come from Dresden and other towns in Lower Saxony.'

The cottage to which Magda took him was set well back from the road, and up against a huge, overhanging sandstone outcrop perhaps 200 feet high. Like most of the other houses in the area, it was a black, timber building, a Czech variant on a log cabin, with white grouting filling the gaps between the timbers and around the window frames. It was one of a dozen or so set along a cinder track.

The back of the cottage was actually built against the rock face, with no space at all between building and rock. From the front and the sides, though, there were sweeping views down across meadows grazed by horses and sheep, all the way to the edge of the forest a mile or two distant. Jake parked in a small bay beside the cottage and they got out to stretch and admire the view.

'Stunning,' Jake said, impressed. 'You can see forever from up here.'

'It was my grandmother's cottage. As a child, I always looked forward to visiting Babička,' Magda said wistfully. 'It is so beautiful here, especially compared to a tenth-floor flat in the city.'

'Which city was that?'

'Prague,' she said with a sigh.

He nodded. So that was where she was from. He had wondered often enough.

'Babička?'

'Grandmother.'

'Ah!'

They stood in silence for a few moments.

'Different to the Algarve, isn't it?' Jake said with a smile.

She just nodded, not bothering to confirm the obvious.

The verdant green was overwhelming. In the Algarve now there was bare earth, rock and sand, and dead looking plants and trees. Here, there were miles of luxuriant, flowing grassland, and the trees were tall and a bright green colour that simply didn't exist in regions with long, hot, rain-free summers.

'It is good growing country, I think,' Magda said. 'For the farmers and the foresters.'

That was self-evidently true.

'Let's hope it's also safe,' Jake said, turning to look at the house.

They spent what was in many ways an idyllic first week there in Vysoká Lípa. It was like being on holiday. They had outrun Fogarty, Bob and anyone else who might be on their trail – the whole damned lot of them! They had escaped unharmed, and were able now to relax and try to recover from their ordeal and flight. There wasn't anyone in the whole world with a clue as to where they were. They were free. Jake liked the feeling that gave him. He liked it a lot.

So they walked in the forest and climbed some low hills covered in pine and beech, and at the end of their walks, there was always a little place where they could buy a cold beer. This was gentle, peaceful country with only a scatter of people living in it permanently, although the weekends always saw an influx of visitors, Germans in the main, but some Czechs, too. No Portuguese, though, Jake pointed out with a smile. And no Brits, thank God!

But seeing a group of German visitors enjoying themselves in a restaurant one evening got Jake thinking about the future. For how much longer would it be possible to cross national borders so easily? Perhaps the journey he and Magda had just made from the Algarve wouldn't be so straightforward before much longer.

Trouble had been brewing on European borders for a year or two. Several million refugees and migrants had arrived, or were on their way, from the Middle East and North Africa, and there was no sign of an end to it. Mostly the influx headed for Germany, following Chancellor Merkel's kindly but perhaps misguided offer to accommodate all who wanted to come. But Greece was in turmoil with them. And Turkey had several million "guests" living in tents.

The Balkan states – Macedonia, Slovenia and so on – as well as Austria and Hungary, had closed their borders at least for a while. Fences were going up. At times, even the French-Belgian border had been closed. What did it all mean? The Schengen agreement, which had opened up the European continent to free travel, was in trouble. That was one thing it meant. It was entirely possible that the twenty year EU experiment of living without internal borders was coming to an end.

Then there was the UK, which wasn't part of Schengen anyway, and now had opted to leave the EU. Jake wondered what it all meant for Magda and himself. They were OK here, certainly at the moment, but how easy was it going to be for them to move and try to do what they had spoken of doing? Perhaps they would find themselves trapped here?

He broached the subject over an evening meal Magda had prepared. A straightforward question seemed a good place to start.

'Have you got a passport, Magda?'

She looked uncertain for a moment, and then shook her head. He wasn't too surprised. It meant she had travelled to Portugal overland, passing through invisible borders effortlessly. She certainly wouldn't have got through an airport without a passport.

'Does it matter?' she asked.

'It does if you want to go to England. And the way things are going, with all the refugees and migrants flooding into Europe, it might soon matter in a lot of other countries, as well.'

'Yes,' she said thoughtfully. 'The borders will become difficult again.'

'Only for people wanting to cross them,' he pointed out with a grim smile.

'So you don't want to stay here?'

'Only for a little while, Magda. We have things to do, remember?'

She smiled. 'I remember.'

He shared out the rest of the wine from the bottle they had bought in the village shop in nearby Jetřichovice, thinking it wasn't bad at all. Drinkable, anyway.

'Velké Bílovice,' he said, peering at the label on the empty bottle.

'It is in Moravia,' Magda told him, 'in the south-east of our country.'

'Not Slovakia?'

She shook her head. 'But they make good wine there, too. Do you have a passport, Jake?'

'I do, but I'm not eager to use it. To get into the UK you have to show your passport, and they have an electronic registering system there now. So they can watch who is entering and leaving the country. It doesn't work perfectly yet. Only eighty-five per cent, the last I heard. But it's getting better.'

'So, Jake, if you return to the UK, that will be on a computer somewhere?'

He nodded. 'And the people who want to kill me could have a way of scanning for my name. Knowing I was back in the UK would give them a better chance of finding me. In fact, if they monitor ferry and airline booking systems, they could even be waiting for me when I arrive.'

Magda looked very thoughtful. Jake just shrugged. But he did know one thing: to have any chance of finding the missing twenty-million quid, never mind warning the others that Fogarty was on their tail, he had to return to the UK and run the gauntlet. Without a passport, though, Magda wouldn't be going with him. Maybe that was a good thing.

'Perhaps it is possible,' Magda said thoughtfully.

'What is?'

'If you had a different passport – one not in your real name – you could go back without them knowing.'

He chuckled. 'If pigs could fly, you mean?'

She looked puzzled.

'It's just an old saying,' he assured her. 'It means "how likely is that?"'

'I see,' Magda said slowly.

Frowning, she added, 'But it is possible, I think. To do that is possible.'

'What is?' he asked again.

'To have such a passport.'

He stopped picking at the label on the empty wine bottle and looked up at her. 'Oh?'

'You can have a new passport,' she said firmly now, 'and so can I. It is no problem, I think.'

He rather thought it was. Sitting here, in glorious isolation in Vysoká Lípa, he couldn't believe it wasn't a problem, but he was prepared to listen to Magda being optimistic.

'How do you work that out?' he asked.

'Easy. We will go to see Mr Phan.'

Chapter 26

Jake had no idea if Petrovice was a good venue for the meeting or not. He just had to trust Magda. Either that or dump her and make his own way back to the UK, and take his chances. As soon as they entered the town, however, he could see that it was ideal.

They came in off the autobahn, a relatively new extension of the E55 that by-passes Dresden and runs on eventually to Prague. A big car park, or open-air market square, off to the right, was the first thing he saw as they entered the town. Then Petrovice was suddenly laid out before them. It was a long street settlement, but more a town than the village he had expected. It was quite a big place.

To his astonishment, there were Asian shops and restaurants on each side as they drove slowly down the main street. What looked from the garish neon signs like Asian hotels and casinos, too. Not your typical provincial Czech town. More an overseas branch of South East Asia.

He chuckled and glanced sideways at Magda. 'Look at it!'

'Vietnamese,' she said with a shrug. 'This is a border town, and the Vietnamese always have their businesses in these places.'

'Vietnamese?' he said with surprise. 'What on earth are they doing here?'

'They called the first ones to come to my country the "Boat People".'

Ah! Of course. The capitalists and their sympathizers who fled in the run-up to the fall of Saigon all those years ago.

'Now their children and grandchildren speak Czech,' Magda added, 'and know no other country.'

'But all these signs and names!'

'It is good for marketing, and perhaps they like to keep alive the memory of their ancestral homeland.'

He thought that was probably right on both accounts. But the way Vietnam had gone, the older folks could be excused if they wondered now why they had ever bothered leaving. These days there didn't seem to be much socialism about the country, or about China, either, for that matter.

Having heard Magda's explanation, he thought the shops and stalls in Petrovice were displaying and advertising exactly the kinds of stuff you might have expected: booze in its infinite varieties, garden gnomes, cigarettes, cheap and colourful clothing – all the usual consumables. Then there were the casinos where you could get rid of any money you had left over from shopping.

'Things are cheaper here than in Germany,' Magda said. 'So German people come to the border towns to shop.'

Jake nodded. Perhaps Germans paid higher taxes – or the Vietnamese were just hot at competitive pricing. Whatever. The result was a hell of a lot of outlets for discount shopping.

Strictly speaking, international borders were not supposed to matter very much these days to the countries in the Schengen area of the EU, but they did still in some places, and in some respects. For the Germans, this would be like Calais and Dunkirk for the Brits. Bargains galore.

'Let's see if your man's here,' Jake suggested, coming back to the reason for their visit.

'He will be,' Magda said tersely.

He hoped so. Magda might trust and believe in him, this Mr Phan, but he certainly didn't. He had no idea who the hell he was. Magda had given him a very good billing, though. She reckoned he was a master craftsman. They would have to see about that. For now, Jake had decided, he would reserve judgement.

They parked the car behind an Asian supermarket. Mid-morning on a slow day in mid-week, and only half a dozen vehicles in the car park. A couple of small, ethnic Vietnamese men were transferring boxes with lurid writing from a shipping container to a trolley, ready to take into the store. Nothing else going on.

'OK?' Magda asked.

Jake nodded.

'It is safe,' she added. 'Don't worry.'

Maybe.

'Let's go see your man,' he said, opening the door. 'And afterwards perhaps we could pick up a couple of phones somewhere around here. We're lost without phones.'

'I agree.'

He smiled as he got out of the car. Magda agreed, did she? How their relationship had changed! Now she seemed to be a fully-fledged partner. What a difference a few days had made.

Magda led the way to a small emergency door at the back of the building. She pressed a buzzer and spoke into an intercom. The door clicked. She opened it. They entered and immediately began to climb a narrow staircase without windows which was lined with promotional posters for Kung Fung-type Asian movies. They all seemed to feature people with hideous expressions and savage martial arts equipment. In the poor light they did nothing for Jake's ease of mind.

On a landing at the top of the stairs, Magda tapped at a door and opened it. Jake followed her inside, still hoping for the best but prepared for something else. He just hoped Magda knew what she was doing. Asian criminal gangs had long arms, and long memories.

He didn't know what to expect on the other side of the door. Perhaps an elderly patriarch; perhaps a gang warrior festooned with weapons. Instead, they were met by a small, sullen man, probably in his thirties, who looked like a bank clerk. The man stared at Jake with great suspicion and made no offer to shake hands. Keeping an eye on Jake, he spoke over his shoulder to Magda in what sounded like the Czech language. Jake tried to appear relaxed.

It was more an interrogation than a greeting, and it went on for a minute or two. The name Petra was mentioned. Petra? Who was that? Then Jake heard his own name, too. Magda stayed calm, if blank-faced, and responded fluently to the questioning. While negotiations continued, Jake wore a friendly smile but stayed alert, ready to respond if a weapon was produced.

After a couple of minutes, Magda turned to Jake and translated some of what had been said.

'This is Mr Phan. He knows me, and trusts me, but he wants to know who you are. I told him you are my partner, and a dear friend. I also told him what we want, and asked if he can provide passports for us.'

Jake nodded his understanding, without taking his eyes from Mr Phan. It was his place, and his move.

Suddenly, Phan surprised him by sticking out a hand and saying in pretty good English, 'Welcome! Any friend of Petra's is my friend also.'

Jake shot a glance at Magda, who shrugged. 'My old name,' she said apologetically.

Jake finally got to shake hands with Phan, who gave him a smile and a little bow before turning to lead them into another room. A young Vietnamese woman was waiting there to serve them tea.

'I will take your photographs in a moment,' Phan said.

Jake began to relax. It looked as though Magda, or Petra, or whatever the hell she was called, seemed to have found them someone who could help. Quite how she had managed that was a question for another time, but it was one he was determined to have answered. Sooner rather than later.

Chapter 27

Magda said she had things to do that morning. So Jake went for a walk alone. That morning, in particular, Dolsky Mlyn, an ancient ruined mill in the nearby Kamenice canyon, looked very special. Breathtakingly beautiful.

He reached the bottom of the long and steep descent via a precipitous defile, and then stood still and let the cool mystery of the place wash over him. The Kamenice River flowed gently by on its way to join the Labe, the river that Magda had told him was known as the Elbe on the other side of the border with Germany. Patches of mist hung over the water and cloaked the stone walls of Dolsky Mlyn on the far side with a romantic haze.

After a while, he sighed and shook himself. It was all very well hiding away here in beautiful Northern Bohemia, but how long could it go on? How long did he want it to go on? Magda seemed happy enough to be here, back on her home turf, and so was he. For the moment at least. But he knew the tranquillity, and the peace, was a bit of an illusion. Nothing had really changed.

By coming here, they had taken their pieces off the board for a time. But it wouldn't stop Fogarty. He wouldn't abandon the search. Jake was sure of that. So far as Fogarty was concerned, he was unfinished business, a man who had helped to bring him down, and a man who just might have the missing millions that he probably considered to be his.

Eventually, and inevitably, perhaps in some now

unimaginable way, their defences would slip. They would grow accustomed to not being in immediate danger. Then one day they would do something stupid or thoughtless, or even accidentally, and that would be it. The roof would crash down. Either that or they would get bored or restless, and leave here because they'd had enough of the tranquillity. Then the wolves would be on their trail once again.

And that was without even considering the £20 million, which was of great interest to a number of people – himself included now. His agreement with Bob wasn't all that important to him, now he knew Bob had been trying deceitfully to use him, but still... Even a small percentage amounted to a healthy chunk of money. It was worth thinking about.

So what was to be done? Stay here, in safe isolation, or return to the real world? He wrestled with that question long and hard, but always came back to the same answer, the one he had worked out in the first place. And it wasn't really to do with the money. It was simply that he knew that if he wanted Fogarty off his back permanently, he would have to return to the arena where Fogarty hunted, and do some hunting himself.

'Go back?' Magda said, when he broached the subject. 'So soon?'

'I think so. The passports should be ready by the end of the week. So Phan said, at least.'

'Then they will be. You can rely on him.'

'Good. Well, once we have them, there's no reason to delay getting on with it. Not for me, at least. But for you, it's different.'

She gave him one of her looks. He didn't even try to interpret it.

'What I mean is you're home now, Magda. This is where you belong, and it's safe here for you. You can stay. You should stay.'

For a moment he thought she was going to spit at him. Instead, she said, 'And that is what you want?'

He shrugged. 'It would be safest for you. That's all I'm thinking. But the decision has to be yours.'

'I belong with you now,' she said sharply. 'Not here. Vysoká Lípa is the past. Where you go, Jake, I go. We have an agreement, don't we?'

He smiled and nodded. 'We do. But I'm not sure you really understand what you're getting into, and how dangerous life will be once we leave here.'

'Phooey!' she said even more sharply. 'We will go together, and do what needs to be done.'

They decided they would collect their new passports and make arrangements to fly to the UK. Probably to London first. There, they would look for Fat Freddie, and hopefully get to him before Fogarty did. After that, it would be a matter of following whatever clues they could find.

Of one thing Jake was sure: there would be clues. Somewhere along the way he would pick up information that would lead him onwards. Hopefully, too, his presence would draw out Fogarty. Risky as it was, he wanted that. Without it, there would be no way of bringing this story to an end.

Chapter 28

The passports were fine, Phan said on the phone. Ready to be picked up now. Jake felt relieved and well satisfied. Phan had done a good job, it seemed. Now they could get on. This holiday, or respite, or whatever it was, was over. The real world awaited their return.

That afternoon Magda went down to the small shop at the bottom of the hill in Vysoká Lípa. There were a couple of things she said she needed to buy. Feminine things, Jake assumed. Women's things. Necessities. They had some travelling ahead of them.

Jake spent a few minutes finishing packing one of two travel bags they had picked up in Petrovice. That was all it took. He wasn't taking much with him. He didn't have much. Nor did Magda. Her bag, on the other side of the bed, also looked packed. He nodded with satisfaction. They would leave early tomorrow and head for the airport on the edge of Prague.

He was restless then, with nothing more to do. Itchy-feet syndrome, he thought with a wry smile. Time to be moving. He left the cottage and set off down the hill to meet Magda. See if she needed any help.

She wasn't in the shop. Jake wasn't surprised about that. What did surprise him was where he found her. She was sitting at a table in the beer garden adjacent to a small restaurant, one of two such places near the bus stop. Two men were with her. The conversation looked to be intense and serious. Magda obviously knew the men, but she didn't look happy. Was that good or bad? One way to find out, Jake thought grimly.

He made his way through the little gateway and across the grassed area towards the table where the three of them sat. 'Here you are!' he said with a smile, addressing Magda but letting his gaze pass across the nearby faces.

Heads and eyes turned towards him.

Both men were dressed casually, but reasonably smart. One looked to be thirty-ish, the other ten or fifteen years older. They both had hard, unsmiling faces. Neither welcomed Jake. The older man, in particular, examined him with frank hostility.

Not friends, then, Jake decided. Not to him or to Magda, judging by the look on her face, and by her silence. What the hell was going on? Trouble, it looked like.

'Magda?' he said. 'Are you going to introduce me to your friends?'

'Of course,' she said, starting to rise to her feet.

The older man grasped her wrist to stop her moving and snapped something in Czech. She slumped back onto her chair.

Not good. Looking dangerous now. Close to out of control, in fact.

The younger man started to get up. Jake grabbed a steak knife from the place setting on an adjacent table, stepped behind the older man and held the knife against his throat.

'Let go of her!'

Nothing happened. The younger man stayed where he was. The older man kept hold of Magda's wrist. Magda's blank face said she was in pain from his grip but was trying not to show it.

Jake repeated his demand.

'Tell him in Czech,' he added, glancing at Magda.

Magda said a few words.

Nothing happened.

Jake waited a moment. Then he pulled the knife back and altered his grip. Without hesitating, he rammed the point of the blade down hard onto the back of the older man's spare hand, which was flat on the table.

Something happened then. Several things, in fact.

The older man cried out with pain and shock, and let go of Magda's wrist. She jerked back out of his reach.

The younger man leapt to his feet, galvanized by Jake's sudden action. A serious looking knife appeared in his hand, and a click locked the blade in place. He turned towards Jake.

Anticipating something like that, Jake had by then let go of the steak knife spearing the older man's hand to the table and brought the Glock pistol out of his pocket.

He levelled the gun at the man with the knife. The man stopped in mid-movement and held back, looking to his partner – perhaps his boss – for guidance. None was forthcoming. The older man was still in shock, frozen by the knife pinning his hand to the table.

'Magda,' Jake said in a level tone, motioning with the pistol. 'Let's go.'

There was a long pause. She seemed to struggle to respond to the instruction, and made no move to stand up. She was locked in place, fastened to her seat. Her eyes were all for the older man, and for the knife pinning his hand to the table.

The older man gathered himself and spoke at last. 'She is going nowhere,' he growled in hesitant English.

Then, with a slow, deliberate movement, he reached out his free hand, took hold of the knife handle and, with a gasp, jerked the blade free.

Magda remained fixed in position, staring at the blood oozing across the table.

'Time to go,' Jake insisted sharply. 'Coming?'

All four of them were still and silent then for a moment.

Unseen forces were at work. The power to compel, and the power to release.

The older man snapped something at her. He called her Petra. She stared at him, visibly confused, stunned and uncertain.

'It's up to you,' Jake said, not knowing himself which way it was going to go. 'Stay, if that's what you want.'

Magda got to her feet then and moved around the table to stand beside him. The man with the bleeding hand said something else to her. She didn't respond.

Jake glanced quickly at her. She nodded. Together then, they backed away from the two men at the table and turned to walk out of the beer garden.

Chapter 29

He said nothing as they walked quickly back up the hill. Nor did she. Instead, they walked so fast they were both pretty breathless, making conversation next to impossible. Once or twice, Jake looked behind. No-one was following.

When they reached the cottage, he said, 'Get your stuff. We're leaving now. If you're coming with me, that is?'

'Give me a couple of minutes, please.'

He grabbed his own travel bag and took it out to the car. When Magda appeared, he waited until she had locked the front door of the cottage before starting the engine. As soon as she was aboard he slipped the clutch and got them moving.

'Jake, I must tell you...'

'Not now. Save it for later.'

They needed to go through Děčín, ten miles or so away. The quickest route was down the hill, past the restaurant where he had found Magda, along the road to Hřensko, and then on into town on the road that ran alongside the river. He didn't go that way. Instead, he headed for Jetřichovice, the start of the long way round. Less obvious.

If they came, they came. But he wasn't going to make it easy for them. From now on, he was taking nothing for granted, and he would take all the precautions he could.

He drove through Děčín, and on to Ústí nad Labem, where they joined the E55 again, the main road to Prague. Only then did he begin to feel like talking.

'So you're still with me?'

'Of course.'

He shook his head. 'Are you sure? Can I be sure?'

'I'm here, aren't I?' she said, flashing him an angry look.

He kept quiet.

'Stop the car!' she demanded. 'I will leave.'

He kept going.

She glared at him. 'Stop the car!'

He took no notice.

She unsnapped the safety belt and threw open her door. With the wind blasting through the car, she screwed herself round. One knee on the seat, and her weight on the foot still on the floor, she braced to hurl herself out of the car.

He braked hard. The sudden deceleration threw her forward, off balance. She struggled back upright and launched herself out of the gaping doorway.

Jake swore, kept his foot hard down on the brake and wrestled with the steering wheel as the lumbering beast of a vehicle bucked and twisted and eventually shuddered to a stop. He leapt out and ran back, leaving the engine running and the Honda nose down on the brink of a ditch. He reached her as she struggled to her feet.

'Get off me!' she screeched as he grasped hold of her.

He kept hold and accepted the pummelling she gave him until she was too weak to hit him any more.

'Magda, Magda!' he soothed her.

'You didn't believe me,' she sobbed, her face scratched and bleeding.

'Forgive me.'

Several cars had passed by now. Another one passed, and hooted. Then an enormous truck gave them a blast on its mighty horn as it roared past, covering them with dust and grit in its wake.

Enough!

He scooped her up and carried her quickly to the Honda. He strapped her in the passenger seat and got back behind the steering wheel. As soon as two more cars had passed, he was able to pull the Honda back onto the road and resume their journey.

'We'll stop for coffee at the next opportunity,' he said. 'I'm sorry,' he added.

She straightened up and pushed her hair back with her fingers, which seemed a good sign. Better, anyway. All in all, she was a bit of a mess. And it's my fault, he thought grimly. I should have handled it better.

They stopped at a service area and headed for the coffee shop. While Jake did the ordering, Magda took herself off to the ladies' toilets.

'That's better!' he said with a rueful smile when she returned. Some urgent repair work had at least stopped the bleeding.

She just shrugged.

But over coffee she gradually came back to him, and began speaking again.

'I have a proposal,' she said.

'Oh?'

'There is a motel here, next to the café. Maybe we could stay here for one night. Then I will tell you everything.'

'Everything?' He nodded. 'It's a deal. Let's finish our coffee first. Then we'll take a look.'

Chapter 30

'So you'd better tell me,' Jake said. 'Who are they? And how dangerous are they?'

They were sitting in their room in the motel, sitting around a low coffee table on dining chairs that were pretty new, and pretty cheap. Probably flat-pack, Jake thought, as his chair wobbled, fit to fall apart every time he moved.

Magda sighed and gazed past him at a bland picture on the wall. Jake waited patiently. He didn't even turn his head to check the picture out. Romantic and historical, probably, like a couple of others he could see. Bohemia in times of yore.

'The man you stabbed is Pavel Kunda. He is a wealthy man from Prague.'

Jake was surprised by the description. 'Wealthy? What does he do?'

'Crime,' she said with a shrug. 'He is a professional criminal.'

Jake shook his head. 'That's a profession in your country?'

'Yes. The same as in England, with your Mr Fogarty.'

Jake gave a wry smile. His Mr Fogarty? Nice.

'How do you know him – or how does he know you?'

Magda hesitated. Either it was very complicated or she didn't want to say.

Jake waited. Might as well have it all out now. He had always known she was a closed book. Back then, he hadn't wanted to open it. Now it was different.

In São Brás he hadn't questioned her because he didn't

want to have to explain himself in return. Now she knew all about him, he needed to know where she was coming from. What she told him would determine if they had a future together.

'This Kunda guy does know you,' he pointed out gently, coaxing her. 'He called you Petra, just like your good friend Mr Phan.'

She tossed her head, indignant. 'My name is Magda now. You know that very well. I am no longer Petra.'

Jake nodded and pressed on with his questioning. 'So how do you know each other, and what did he want with you back there?'

'It is complicated.'

'Take your time. Until we get hungry, there's no need for us to leave this room.'

She gave him a faint smile, which did nothing to relieve the tension in the room.

'I told you I grew up in Prague, which is technically true. But my parents split up and moved away when I was quite young. So I lived with my grandmother in Vysoká Lípa for a few years. Then, after I left school, I moved back to Prague to find work.

'At first, I stayed with an aunt, who had a spare room in her flat. It was very exciting for me to be there at that time in my life, in such a big city. The tramcars. The shops. The theatres. So many people – and such exciting people!

'I found work in a kavárna, a small café, and that was where I met Pavel Kunda. He lived nearby and used to come into the shop every day for coffee, and for koláček – little cakes. He was quite a lot older than me, but he was glamorous seeming and amusing, and he always had money. Most of all, he liked me, and paid me much attention. In time, he became my first boyfriend.'

Jake almost wished he hadn't opened the book. He wasn't sure he wanted to know Magda's life history – not right now, at least. He just wanted to know who the guy he had stabbed was, and how much of a threat he was going to be.

'Was he a criminal back then?'

Magda nodded. 'Oh, yes. That was why he had money. He did all sorts of things to earn it. Not sophisticated things, you understand, but the kind that gave him a good living.'

Good living? Jake thought. Well, that was one way of looking at it.

'At first, I didn't know he was like that,' Magda resumed. 'But soon I did, and it seemed OK.' She shrugged and added, 'I don't deny it. I liked the life. I was young, and it was exciting. Then when he suggested I work for him, I liked that, too.'

'What did you do?' asked Jake, interested now despite himself.

She shrugged. 'Not much to start with, but soon Pavel realized there were things I was good at. I had a good brain. I could remember things, and I was good at numbers. So he used me to keep the books and help run the business.'

'The criminal business?'

'Of course. But there was more. Pavel gradually acquired legal businesses, too. Restaurants, bars, clubs, and such things. Someone had to manage them. Increasingly, it became me.'

Jake wondered what the criminal enterprises were but decided not to ask. There wasn't time. Anyway, he doubted if there would be many surprises there, but he was wrong about that.

'After a time, the business became international,' Magda continued. 'There were guns, of course.'

'Of course?'

'Well, this country, Bohemia, has always made many guns. It is natural that they are sold to people in other countries. And not every buyer is a government, yes?'

Jake shrugged. 'I suppose so. Where is this leading, Magda? Can we speed it up a bit?'

She might have pouted indignantly at that, but she didn't. Instead, she gave him the inscrutable stare she always used when she felt he needed putting in his place. It told him she was getting back to normal.

'You are hungry so soon?' she asked waspishly. 'You want to finish our discussion already?'

'Sorry, sorry! No, of course not. Carry on, please.'

After a dignified pause, she said, 'One important international contact Pavel made was your friend Mr Fogarty.'

'Ah!'

She nodded. 'Yes, indeed. Things were done, arrangements made. A relationship established. Guns were exported, as well as other things. Later, a new trade developed, a very profitable one for both sides. It concerned money.'

Jake could see now where this was going. She had said in the beginning that it was complicated. Complicated things took time to explain. He should have been more patient.

'Money laundering, perhaps?'

Magda nodded. 'I believe that is what it is called in your language.'

My language now, is it, Jake thought grimly. She really was right back into it. The persona developed in the Algarve, for the moment at least, had been shelved. More fool me for ever trusting her.

'Pavel used me a lot for that new trade.' She shrugged. 'The numbers again, and also I could speak and understand English. Those things were very useful now he had entered a new business relationship with Mr Fogarty.'

The more she spoke, the more he realized how very little he had ever known about her. It had suited him back then to know, and ask, nothing about her background. Now he was learning how big a mistake that had been. He just hoped it wasn't going to get him killed.

'How did Kunda and Fogarty get to know each other?'

She shrugged again. 'Some things I never knew, even though I lived with Pavel and believed I was trusted. So I became the trusted person who would go to London and bring back to Prague a sample of the money that was to be laundered. Not enough money to arouse suspicions if I was ever stopped, which happened once or twice, but just enough for Pavel to assess the value.'

'Not too new, and not too old, presumably?'

'Yes. That determined the price. Sometimes the bank notes would be in such poor condition that Pavel would not accept them.'

'What happened to them, then?'

'Perhaps Fogarty just burned them?'

Jake smiled. Somehow he couldn't see it. Fogarty would likely have had back-up arrangements, at an appropriate price.

'But that was unusual,' Magda continued. 'Mostly, the quality was acceptable, and allowed Pavel to set a price he could propose to Fogarty.'

'What happened after that? How was the money moved out of England?'

She shrugged. 'I don't know. That was not my business. I just did my part. Then other people became involved, and I was happy to let them get on with it.

'These trips to London were very stressful for me, especially as my relationship with Pavel deteriorated. So I didn't want to know any more. I didn't care. You understand?'

Well, maybe. Jake decided to let it go for now.

'Who did you deal with in England? Not Fogarty himself, presumably?'

She shook her head. 'Never. Usually it was his main man, as Pavel called him. Mr Hendrik?'

'I don't know.'

It could have been Hendrik, though. Bob had mentioned that name. Fogarty's chief of staff, he'd called him.

'Sometimes there was another man. I never knew his name. I just called him Mr Little, because he was small and dark. But now I believe it may have been the man you call Nicci – the Greek person.'

Jake nodded. He wouldn't be surprised.

'So where were you the night the roof fell in, when I was involved and it all went wrong?'

'Pavel always told me to be watchful, and to leave immediately if I felt anything was wrong. There were escape routes arranged for me. I took one, when I became concerned, and left.'

Jake shook his head with growing amazement. It was hard to believe, but he was going to have to get used to it. This woman, who he had picked up on the Algarve so innocently, had been right there in the middle of it all. Their meeting had not been an accident at all. She had been pointed at him right from the start.

'So you were there, at the scene? In the Team Valley?'

She shook her head. 'No. Nearby, in a hotel like this one. I did not receive the phone call I expected. Also, there were many sirens and police cars. I left early,' she finished with another of her shrugs.

So, Jake thought. Several things were making sense now. And several other things were deeply troubling.

'You must be the rather mysterious Russian woman I heard about?'

'So it seems.' She smiled. 'English people are not very good at foreign languages, are they? But it suited me for them to think I was Russian.'

Chapter 31

'So what else do you want to know?' Magda asked.

'Now we come to the part about what you were doing in the Algarve with me. And then you can tell me how you ended up with those two guys back at the restaurant in Vysoká Lípa. That should keep us going for a little while – unless you want to break now, and go and get something to eat?'

Magda shook her head. 'No. It is better if I explain everything now.'

'Fair enough.'

Jake was trying to stay calm and reasonable. For the moment, all he wanted were the facts. He would process them in due course, and think then about what they meant. But right now it was the simple, unadorned facts he wanted.

He was beginning to realize how deep was his ignorance of a great many things, Magda in particular. He had always been aware that he knew very little about her, but that hadn't seemed to matter. Now he was having to face up to the fact that there were two Magdas: the one he had lived with in the Algarve, and the professional criminal he had heard others refer to as "the Russian woman". It seemed unlikely that they could be reconciled.

He was beginning to wonder, too, just how badly he had got things wrong, and what the consequences still might be. It was obvious now that his linking up with Magda hadn't been at all fortuitous, whatever he had thought at the time.

'Tell me what you were doing in the Algarve, Magda. Why were you there?'

'Pavel sent me there to watch you, and to try to discover if you had the stolen money.'

'I see.'

So it was every bit as bad as he had been starting to think. His relationship with Magda had not begun accidentally. It had been manufactured by a criminal mastermind based in Prague.

Wonderful, bloody marvellous! Nothing like the truth to make you feel good about yourself. And she had told him so straightforwardly, as well. No attempt at all to butter him up or sugar-coat the plain unadorned fact that he had been seeking.

Staring hard at her, trying to remain calm, he said, 'What have you told him?'

'The truth.' She shrugged. 'I soon told him you were living a simple life in the Algarve, and that there was nothing at all to suggest you had much money.'

'And he bought that?'

'He said to keep watching. So I did for a time, and then I didn't bother any more. I just said I would stay in Portugal for a while. Pavel didn't care by then. We had grown apart, and he had plenty of other girls, younger girls.'

That sounded honest, too. Whether it really was, or not, he couldn't tell yet.

'Then what?'

'Jake, you know the rest!' she said with exasperation, her stone-face disappearing for the first time. 'We met properly, and then we began living together. We were happy, and we cared for each other. We had a good life.'

'We did, didn't we?' he said with a bitter chuckle.

Was that a tear she had just shed? He rather thought it was, but he wasn't going to let that fool him.

'And we can again,' she said.

'Is that what you think? Well, perhaps. So what about that

cosy little scene this afternoon in Vysoká Lípa? How did that come about?'

'Pavel was aware that Fogarty was out of prison, and searching for the missing money. So he got his own people to join in. I think he wanted to satisfy himself that I was telling the truth about you.'

'How did he know we were here, in this country?'

Magda shrugged, leaving him to figure it out for himself. It wasn't difficult.

'And what about your meeting with him? How did that happen?'

'He phoned me to arrange it.'

Grim-faced, Jake said, 'He phoned you?'

She nodded.

'On the phone you no longer have?'

She buried her face in her hands.

'Where is it?'

Magda reached into a pocket and brought out a small, slim phone. She laid it on the coffee table.

Jake stared at it wearily. Now he knew how it had been possible for Fogarty to track them. For all he knew, Fogarty could even be right here in the Czech Republic.

Probably not, though, he decided on second thoughts. Kunda wouldn't accept that. This was his territory. Fogarty would probably just have handed over responsibility for this leg of the hunt.

Magda picked up the phone and removed the sim card. She ground it beneath her heel and dropped the phone in the waste bin.

'A bit late,' Jake said heavily, 'but it's a start, I suppose.'

'What will we do now?'

It was a good question. What would they do now?

'Let's go and get something to eat.'

Chapter 32

They were quiet over their meal in the restaurant adjacent to the hotel. Jake had a lot to think about and Magda was subdued. He suspected she was emotionally exhausted, which he wasn't far from being himself. It had turned into one hell of a day.

At least some things made more sense now, though, Jake thought ruefully. That people had been able to track their movements in the Algarve, and then find them here, had been baffling and very worrying. Now he knew how it had been done. That felt like progress.

Another thing that made sense at last was how and why Magda could cope admirably in situations that might have been expected to completely unhinge a normal young woman with no experience of the rougher side of life. She had been astonishingly calm and clear-headed when faced with some pretty damned appalling events. Now he could explain it. She was a seasoned warrior.

What he was struggling with now was if, when and where he should dump her. He knew he couldn't afford to be sentimental. She had let him down, betrayed him even. She had shared his bed on a false promise, and she had misled him big-time for far too long. Somehow he had survived – so far. But he couldn't trust her any more. Realistically, they had reached the end of the road.

Before he told her so, though, he wanted to get from her whatever he could in the way of information that might help him survive a bit longer. Then it would be Arrivederci, baby!

Hell. For all he knew, she might even be pleased when he told her. She could go back to fucking Pavel then – in more ways than one!

'So what now, Jake?' Magda asked as she sipped her coffee at the end of the meal.

He took his time answering. 'I'm not sure. What about Kunda? What will he do now?'

'It is very simple.' She gave another of her exquisite shrugs. 'He will try to kill you, and me. And he will continue looking for the missing money.'

Put like that, it was simple. Once again, but reluctantly now, he had to admire Magda's capacity for clear-headed thinking. No nonsense, or obfuscation, at all. She just said it how it was.

'Me, I can understand,' Jake said, 'after what I did to him back there. But you, too?'

'Yes. I know him. I betrayed him when I came with you.'

Ah! I was forgetting that, Jake thought. That's a complication. Maybe I need to think again.

He changed the subject. 'Is Kunda tied in with Fogarty?'

Head on one side, she considered for a moment. 'I think not. Not in the sense I believe you mean. They are occasional collaborators, with certain shared interests, but they are certainly not partners. They are both looking for the missing money, but independently of each other.

'One other thing. Because Fogarty has been in prison, and now is on the run, he is… How do you say? Dead in the water?'

Jake nodded.

'Dead in the water,' she said with satisfaction at having got it right. 'Fogarty cannot manoeuvre now like he did before. He has influence still, and he has resources. But so has Pavel, and Pavel is legally a free man. He can go anywhere openly. So he will proceed alone, I believe, and follow his own best interests.'

'So,' Jake mused, 'we and the others – and the money – now have two independent organizations hunting us? Is that how you see it?'

Magda nodded. 'But it is too late for two of your former colleagues. One man in Yorkshire and another in Scotland have been killed already.'

'Kunda told you?'

'Yes. They knew nothing about the money,' she said with a shrug, 'and eventually they died. Pavel told me. I believe him.'

Jake grimaced and looked away. So that was Penrose and Gregory he no longer had to worry about. Christ, there aren't many left on that damned list!

And no wonder, he reflected, that Magda was in a bad place when he found her in the beer garden. She had had even more to worry about than he knew. It wasn't at all surprising that she had seemed so hesitant and confused.

She knew a lot, too. He couldn't ignore or deny that.

'OK,' he said briskly, knowing now what he needed to do. 'Here's the plan. That is, if you are still with me?'

'Yes, I am, Jake. You should know that.'

Well, maybe. He would have to think more about that, and wait to see what happened. But things were different now. Total trust was out the window. He could no more trust Magda absolutely than believe in fairies after today's revelations.

'The plan then,' he said with more confidence than he really felt, 'is we simply carry on. We do what we had intended to do. We can't ignore today – at least, I can't – but maybe we can put it behind us. So we will go to Petrovice tomorrow, and pick up our passports and a couple of new phones. Then we'll go to England. Is that OK with you?'

'It is.'

He could hear the relief in her voice. He placed his hand on top of hers. 'You and me,' he said softly. 'Together.'

Looking directly at him, she gave a little smile and said, 'Thank you, Jake.'

Chapter 33

London was cool, damp and overcast. Inevitably, they shivered when they left the plane, and shivered even more when they left the Heathrow terminal. Magda gave him a brave smile. He thought he knew how she felt. It wasn't like the Algarve, or Northern Bohemia, either.

'Welcome to England, Mrs Robinson,' he said confidently. 'You'll soon get used to the weather.'

'Thank you, Mr Robinson. Always have I wanted to come to England. I will not even notice the weather.'

'That's the spirit!'

They were the Robinsons now, supposedly from somewhere he'd never heard of in the West Midlands, according to their rather scuffed new passports. Phan had done a good job. The passports had got them through the lines at both Prague and Heathrow airports. Money well spent, even if it had been hard not to wince at the price.

As the Robinsons, they took a cab into Bayswater, where they checked into a small hotel that had what they needed: bed, food and quiet. Phan had also provided them with several throw-away phones, and Jake soon began working one of them. His first call went to Bob. It was time to start work.

'You're back, bonnie lad! So where've you been?'

'Taking a break, Bob. There were some difficulties we had to overcome.'

'We? Who's we?'

Jake winced.

'Just a figure of speech. Me, I and all those who provided help along the way.'

'Oh, aye?'

He grimaced. Bob was suspicious. But he was damned if he was going to pander to his suspicions. It was better that he knew nothing about Magda. Better, actually, that nobody knew about her.

'Fat Freddie,' Jake said. 'Tell me what you've got on him.'

'So you're in London?'

'I don't think I said that, did I?' He sighed and added, 'Oh, it's not you, Bob. It's just that the former colleagues seem to be dropping like flies, and the way I was traced in Portugal makes me suspicious of all phones, including yours.'

'So you've heard about Penrose and Gregory, have you?'

'Yeah. I'm not taking any chances.'

'Fair enough. Look after yourself, bonnie lad. Be careful. Stay alive.'

'I'll do that. So what have you got for me?'

Pretty much all Bob had was an address where Fat Freddie had been living a year previously. Jake doubted if he would be there now, but it was somewhere to start.

The building was in Barnet. It was a block of flats that had seen good days since it was built in the 1960s, but probably not many. They called into a café across the road for a coffee. From the table where they sat, they had a good view of Acadia Towers.

Jake counted twelve floors above ground, and it looked as though there was parking and utilities below ground. The address for Freddie was flat 608, halfway up the building. That would be Witness Protection's idea of a pragmatic compromise. Freddie had a choice if danger threatened of making for either the roof or the ground floor. Or, if Fogarty caught up with him, he would be going out the window, with no choice at all.

'It is not a nice place, I think,' Magda observed as she slowly stirred sugar into her black coffee.

'Man on the run wouldn't care about that.'

'Will he recognize you?'

Jake shrugged. 'Maybe, maybe not. I only ever saw him a couple of times. But I'm sure he'll listen to what I have to say. It's in his interests.'

Magda nodded.

They finished their coffees. They wouldn't learn anything else from sitting there sipping Americanos, Jake decided. Time to go see Fat Freddie.

Surprisingly, although there was free access to the building, the lift still worked. He pressed for the seventh floor, the one above Freddie's. Magda saw him do it but didn't say anything. She seemed to know what he was doing, which was no surprise to Jake. He knew now she was no amateur with a natural talent for this kind of thing. She was an experienced professional with a lot of miles on the clock. He was getting used to the idea.

The lift came to a stop. They got out. Jake turned to head for the emergency stairs. The staircase stank. It smelled, and looked, as if it was being used as both a bedroom and a toilet, even at that height above the street. He held his breath as they tiptoed through the bedding, accumulated rubbish and everything else. Magda said nothing but she wore that stony look he was used to seeing when something displeased her.

When they emerged onto the floor below, she broke her silence. 'English people!'

He shrugged and said, 'Not necessarily. Lots of foreigners here, these days.'

She humphed and said, 'No Czech would live like that.'

Jake kept quiet.

'Do you still want me with you?'

'Yes, if you don't mind. Seeing a woman at his door, instead of a man on his own, Freddie will feel less threatened – if he's there, that is.'

The door of flat 608 opened promptly when he pressed the button for the doorbell. A young woman appeared. She looked surprised.

'Oh, hello! Have you been standing there long? The bell doesn't work, I'm afraid.'

Jake shook his head and smiled. 'No. We've just arrived.'

'To see me? Are you from the agency?'

Again he shook his head. 'We're here to see Mr Rogers. Is he in?'

'There's no-one here with that name. You've got the wrong flat. Oh, wait a minute!'

She turned and disappeared for a moment. When she returned, she had a bundle of envelopes in her hand that she was scanning.

'Yes. I thought I recognized the name. Rogers was the previous tenant. These are for him. Bills, I think. He's been gone nearly a year now, but he didn't leave a forwarding address and he's never made contact with me.'

She finished with a shrug. 'I've just kept them on the table in the hall.'

'Return to sender?' Jake suggested with a smile.

Her face lit up. 'Oh, are you an Elvis fan?'

He laughed and thanked her for her time. Then they left.

'In a way,' he said to Magda, as they waited for the lift, 'I'm glad we didn't find Freddie there. If we had, he probably wouldn't have been alive.'

Magda didn't seem bothered by that possibility.

'What did she mean about Elvis?'

'It was just a joke.'

After a moment's pause, Magda said, 'I don't understand English jokes. They are not funny, I think.'

Afterwards, he thought long and hard about how they might find Fat Freddie. There would be a trail. There always was. It was just a matter of finding the end of it, and then hanging on and following it.

Money could be the key. Money paid and money spent. Money owed, money recorded. Once there was money involved, somewhere there would be a record. How to find it?

'Ask your friend, Bob?' Magda suggested.

He shook his head. 'No. I prefer to keep him out of it for the moment.'

'You don't trust him?' she asked with a smile. 'You don't trust your friend?'

'I don't trust anyone,' he said. 'It's better to minimize the number of people who know what we're doing.'

'Do you trust me?' she asked softly.

He chuckled and said, 'Implicitly!'

It was a blatant lie, and she probably knew it. He certainly didn't trust Magda, not really. Not now. Even without the recent revelations he probably wouldn't have trusted her fully. He'd known too little about her.

As it was now, he would keep her with him, so far as that turned out to be possible, mainly because she was useful to him. She knew things he didn't. She knew more about the principal actors in this drama than he did. Some of them, she knew personally, and she knew a lot about how they operated. All that was worth a lot to him.

As for the rest of it, well, although he certainly didn't want Kunda exacting revenge from her, he didn't really know if she was with him or not. But that didn't matter. She had fooled him once; it wouldn't happen again.

'We should sit down and talk more about ourselves,' Magda said sadly. 'Then perhaps we could trust each other more.'

So she didn't trust him any more than he trusted her?

With a relaxed smile, he said, 'That's a very good idea, Magda. One of these days we should do just that.'

146

Chapter 34

It was strictly a business meeting. They sat in their hotel room, armed with mugs of strong coffee, and considered how best to find Fat Freddie. By then, Jake was not overly anxious about Freddie's welfare. The man had slipped away from the flat where he had been living long ago, and it was hard to believe he would be unaware of the threat Fogarty posed now he'd escaped.

Besides, he couldn't pretend to have liked the man. He had hardly known him. Just another professional criminal in the circles in which Bob moved. More on his mind was the idea that perhaps, just perhaps, Fat Freddie knew where the money was. That was a good enough reason to continue searching for him.

'What have you got there?' he asked as Magda pulled a sheaf of paper out of her bag.

'I thought it might help,' she said, handing over a small pile of envelopes, fliers and sundry bits of paper.

He read the address on the top envelope and then just stared at the pile with astonishment. 'I didn't see you take them.'

She shrugged. 'Maybe they will reveal something.'

'Good thinking,' Jake said thoughtfully, riffling through the pile. 'I did wonder about them. I even thought of going back to the flat for them, when the woman wasn't there.'

'She doesn't know who we are,' Magda said, anticipating his next point. 'So what could she do anyway?'

'Not much,' he admitted. 'You're right. It wouldn't really have mattered whether she was there or not.'

He wondered for a moment how on earth Magda had managed it without him or the woman noticing. Obviously, she had served a good apprenticeship.

He was grudgingly impressed, too, by how her mind worked. It wasn't the first time she had displayed an uncanny knack of thinking useful thoughts.

In fact, Magda – or whatever the hell her name was! – was just full of surprises. And she was certainly earning her keep.

'Well, let's get started.' Handing back half the pile of papers, he said, 'See what you make of these. I'll take this half. Then we can swap over. Two brains are better than one.'

They went through the two piles in silence, opening envelopes and studying the contents, unwrapping the fliers and notices. Then they sat back and considered. Magda made some more coffee before they started comparing notes.

'No bank statements,' Jake said for openers. 'In fact, nothing from a bank, or any other financial organization. That suggests Freddie's departure from the flat was a planned strategic withdrawal rather than a panicked evacuation.'

'He may not have used a bank,' Magda pointed out. 'For a man like him, using cash would be safer.'

He thought about that for a moment. It was a good point. Was it possible? Paying for everything with cash? Well, maybe. Especially if the rent for the flat was being paid by the Witness Protection programme. He'd have to ask Bob about that.

'He likes flowers,' Magda pointed out, lifting a couple of invoices from a florist out of the pile.

He nodded. 'Odd, that. What would he want with them? Anyway, he must have been pretty relaxed about his situation to be ordering flowers. Anything else strike you?'

She shook her head.

So they hadn't got much. Just confirmation that Freddie hadn't fled in a blind panic, and a suggestion that he liked flowers.

Magda said, 'Being fat, maybe he has health problems and needs medication?'

'What makes you think he's fat?' he asked with a smile. 'Just because I call him Fat Freddie doesn't mean he's fat. It's just a rude name I use for him.'

'So is he fat?'

'Yes.'

She laughed and shook her head. 'You English!'

'Besides,' Jake pointed out, 'lots of fat people – most fat people, in fact – don't need medication.'

Magda just shrugged.

But she'd got him thinking. Freddie wasn't just overweight. He was pretty damned obese. People with that condition often did develop other issues. And people with health problems, especially those with plenty of time on their hands, tended to visit their doctor and get prescriptions for things they hoped would help.

Furthermore, people like that would be less likely to pick up their prescriptions from the far side of the city. They would be more inclined to stay local, mobility and breathing difficulties reining them in. Maybe that was Freddie? He pulled out his phone and started doing some Googling.

'What are you doing?' Magda asked.

'I'm looking for local chemists – pharmacists. We can visit them, and see if they have a prescription for Freddie we can pick up for him.'

Magda nodded and looked thoughtful. Then she made a suggestion of her own. 'First,' she said, 'why not ask your friend Bob if Freddie had health problems?'

He hadn't thought of that. Magda again.

He sent Bob a text, asking him to email a copy of anything he could find on Freddie's health condition. There would be something. Any programme as bureaucratic as Witness Protection was bound to have a personnel file for each of its clients.

Rather than just sit and wait for Bob's response, he made a list of the pharmacies located within a mile of Freddie's old flat. Then they set off to visit them.

His thinking was that although Freddie might have a doctor on the other side of London – possibly in Essex, even – he would probably collect his repeat prescriptions, if there were any, from somewhere close to where he lived. Not necessarily, of course. But it was worth a shot.

The young woman behind the counter of the first shop they visited was very helpful when he explained what they wanted.

'He's not very well,' Jake said with a wry smile. 'He can't go far from a toilet. So he asked us to pick up his prescription for him.'

'There's a lot of it about at the moment, stomach upsets,' the woman said sympathetically. 'Let me just check. Mr Jenkinson, you said?'

'Yes, that's right. He says it's because we had a mild winter. Didn't kill all the germs.'

'I've heard that before,' she assured him. 'Address?'

He gave her the address of Freddie's old flat. She was very helpful and had a good look, but she couldn't find anything for Freddie.

'I'll call the GP's surgery,' she decided. 'And see what's happened to it.'

Jake shook his head. 'Thanks, but don't bother. It's not urgent. We'll call back again a bit later.'

'Are you sure?' she asked, looking concerned.

He nodded. 'I don't know the name of his GP anyway.'

'Well...'

'We'll call back,' he said firmly.

She nodded and turned to deal with another customer, an elderly woman who looked as if she should be in a hospital bed rather than a chemist's shop. She looked far more deserving than Fat Freddie was anyway.

'The next shop?' Magda asked when they got outside.

He nodded.

They visited five pharmacies without success. None of them had a prescription waiting for Freddie to collect. But none of them challenged their right to collect a prescription for him, if they'd had one. So the plan might have worked.

'Coffee?' Jake suggested after they left the fifth shop.

'Strong coffee,' Magda said. 'With sugar. I need more energy.'

'Oh, my! Start taking sugar, and you'll need a prescription yourself.'

'Only if I become Fat Magda – or Big Bertha.'

'I don't think that's going to happen,' he assured her.

She grinned. Then his phone vibrated, as the reply from Bob came in.

Chapter 35

'This is interesting,' Jake said, as he scanned the pages of text Bob had sent, and ignored Bob's query as to why he wanted them.

Magda sat still and waited patiently.

'Freddie's health report. He wasn't in terribly good shape.'

'No?'

'Heart trouble, arthritis, Type 2 diabetes, and he was waiting for a hip replacement. So he certainly will be on prescription medication – painkillers, and everything else. We've been thinking along the right lines. I wonder who his doctor is, or was – if he was ever registered with one.'

He passed the phone over to Magda to look at and took a sip of coffee while he mulled the information over. Would the programme have fixed Freddie up with a GP registration, or would they have left it for him to do himself? He'd better ask Bob. Either way, there had to be doctor involved.

Where would the practice be located? The problem was that once Freddie had decided to go off the radar, he might well have abandoned all his commitments and registrations, including the medical. Not to have done so would have been pretty stupid.

That would have meant losing his place in the queue for a hip operation, presumably, but so what? His life was more valuable than his hip. Anyway, if he did have any of the money from the heist that was still floating around, he wouldn't need the NHS. He could go straight to Harley Street.

'So,' Magda said thoughtfully, 'a very fat, middle-aged man with heart problems and arthritis pain who needs a new hip.'

'That just about sums Freddie up,' Jake admitted with a wry smile.

Wearing what he was coming to think of as her inquisitorial look, Magda said, 'So how did he move about the city? We know he didn't have a car. That woman said so.'

Jake frowned, wondering what she was getting at.

'Well, he wouldn't have done much walking, that's for sure. Public transport, presumably – buses and the tube.'

'Perhaps not, if he has the money.'

He stared at her. 'What are you thinking?'

'I am thinking taxis.'

Taxis? Regular taxis? Shit! He hadn't thought of that.

'Let's look for local taxi companies,' he said, reaching out a hand to reclaim his phone.

They found three within a couple of miles of Freddie's old flat. Two were quite close, one some distance away.

'I'll take the one furthest away,' he said. 'Can you visit the other two?'

'Of course.'

Magda pushed her chair back, ready to get going.

'Hang on!' he protested. 'I can see you're keen, but I haven't finished my coffee yet.'

She grinned and waited patiently. He shook his head.

The company Jake visited, Alpha Plus Cabs, looked the part. He nodded with satisfaction as he rounded the corner and the office came into view. He could imagine Freddie using this one. Sandwiched between a kebab shop and a dog grooming parlour, it wasn't any bigger than a newspaper kiosk. But five black cabs were stood on the street outside waiting for business, their drivers in a group, chatting beneath a haze of cigarette smoke.

The young guy running the office was on the phone when Jake went inside. His spare hand was poised to pick up another phone as soon as he was finished with the current call.

'How can I help?' he asked when he was done.

'I've just taken over a flat from a guy who was one of your regular clients.'

'One of our regular clients?' the man repeated with a smile.

'I need to contact him, but I don't have his new address. I assume you always invoice him for your services?'

The man was shaking his head already. 'We don't do that – not for anybody. Either you pay cash or you don't ride.'

'OK. I've got that wrong. But you do have regular clients?'

'A few. What's the name and address?'

Jake told him.

The man shook his head. 'He's not with us. Sorry. We don't go there.'

Already he was reaching for a ringing phone. Busy guy. Busy business. But he seemed in full control. He would certainly know if Freddie had been a regular client.

Another dead end. Jake just hoped Magda had done better.

On the way back to the hotel, he detoured to take another look at the block of flats where Freddie had rested for a while under Bob's so-called protection. That place was still the only firm link they had to Freddie. Maybe seeing it again would spark another idea.

He did more than look at the place. He ventured inside the building and managed to get into Freddie's old flat as well. The woman, the tenant who had succeeded Freddie, had cleared out and gone now. That much was evident from the gaps where furniture had once stood, and from the empty wardrobe and chest of drawers that had been left behind.

He poked around but found nothing of interest. Certainly no trace of Freddie.

As he left the building, he noticed an elderly man in a boilersuit sweeping the entrance to the underground car park. He nodded at him. Then, on impulse, he paused to have a word with him.

'Hi! You look after the place?'

'Just the car park. Not the main building.'

'Been here a while?'

'A few years now. Five or six, I think. Why?'

'You might be able to help me. Do you know a Mr Jenkinson?'

'Freddie?' The man chuckled. 'Of course I do. Grand chap, Fat Freddie.'

Jake smiled encouragingly. 'I was wanting to talk to him but I don't seem to be able to catch him in.'

'No, you won't. Not here, you won't. He's been gone a while.'

'Left, you mean?'

'That's right. A few months ago now. Maybe longer.'

'That's a pity.'

'You're right there! It is. He was going to sell me his old car when he got his new one. Not that that would ever have really happened.'

Jake was surprised. The woman in the flat had said she didn't think Freddie had a car. Had that been wrong?

'Why not?' he asked. 'Why wouldn't he have sold you it?'

'A car like that? A classic Series 3 BMW? Freddie thought more of that car than any of the women he used to bring here. Spent hours polishing and tinkering with it down here. In fact, it hardly ever left the garage. Not worth it in London, he used to say. Either someone would nick it or they would bang into it deliberately, just out of spite. Besides, what with the congestion charge, and one thing and another...'

The wheels inside Jake's head were spinning. Possible answers to questions were popping up on all sides.

'Ladies' man, was he, Freddie?'

'I'll say!' the caretaker said with a chuckle. 'You might not think it, but he was.'

Perhaps that explained the florist's invoices, if not how Freddie had got around town.

'How did he travel, if he didn't use his car? Taxis?'

The man shook his head. 'He wouldn't use them. A right rip-off, he used to say. No, I used to let him use my motor.

It's only an old Ford, but it's a decent enough car. A Mondeo, you know?'

Jake nodded, as if he did know. Anything to keep the confidences coming.

'Freddie used to pay me for it. Anyway, I have my bus pass. So I don't very often need it myself. It's just that I've always had a car, and I wouldn't like to be without one now. Out of interest, you know? That's why I have this job, really. And it was why Freddie used to say he would sell me his BMW. He would want it to go to a good home!'

The man chuckled and shook his head, visibly entertained still by thought of past conversations with Fat Freddie.

'It was in good nick, obviously?' Jake pressed.

'I should say so.'

The man went on to tell him, unasked, that it was black. He even knew its registration number. Freddie's car had clearly made a big impression on him. Jake committed the information to memory and began to draw the conversation to a close.

'I don't suppose you know where he moved to?'

The man shook his head. 'But I'll ask him if he drops round to see me one of these days. I'll tell him you were looking for him. What did you say your name was?'

Jake gave him a name, somebody's name. It wasn't worth giving him his own. Freddie wouldn't be back here. Nor would the BMW. Freddie wouldn't be driving it much, either. He was pretty astute. It sounded like his cherished car was one to attract attention. He wouldn't want that.

Jake asked the man to give Freddie his name and phone number if he did show up, and gave him twenty quid for his trouble. Given that the name and phone number were both fictitious, the arrangement wasn't going to do him much good. Even so, that twenty quid turned out to be a good investment.

Jake's phone went off just as he was taking his leave. He glanced at the screen. Magda. He pressed the button.

'Get out, Jake – now! They're coming down the street.'

It was a shock but he didn't question her. Automatic flight response. He turned, ready to sprint for the street. Several figures were running along the pavement.

The car park attendant had seen them, too. He grabbed Jake's sleeve. 'That way!' he snapped, pointing back into the car park. 'It'll be safer. Use the fire escape.'

No time to consider, or ask why. Jake took the advice and headed into the darkened interior of the building's basement below ground. Then he followed the chain of emergency lights that led to the emergency staircase and an emergency door. He burst through, back into daylight, just as his phone buzzed again.

'Go left!' Magda snapped. 'I've got the car.'

He raced down the back lane without looking back to see if he was being followed.

Fifty yards in front of him, the car they had hired swung into view and screeched to a halt. He raced up to it. The passenger door flew open. He threw himself inside. The car took off with a screech of abused rubber. Jake pulled his legs and hands clear as the door slammed shut, powered by the speed of the turn.

No gunshots had been fired.

That was his overriding thought as they sped away.

Chapter 36

After a few minutes of some pretty crazy high-speed driving, and having been thrown all over the place, Jake began to relax. 'Thanks,' he said.

He'd had no idea Magda could drive like that. It was something else to make him think.

Magda nodded, flashed him a quick smile and glanced once more in the rear-view mirror. 'I think we are OK now,' she said.

'Thank God for that! Who were they?'

'I can't be sure.'

'A guess, then.'

She shrugged. 'Probably Kunda's people. But they might be with Fogarty, I suppose.'

So Magda didn't know any more than he did who they were. So what? He knew they had two gangs after them now. It didn't really matter which of them had been on his tail back there. But how had it happened? Accident, or what?

'How did they get onto me, I wonder?'

It was a rhetorical question but Magda took it seriously. 'Probably someone told them you were visiting Freddie's flat,' she said. 'Someone they paid to tell them if something like that ever happened.'

He nodded. Possibly. He had nothing better to suggest.

'I'm not going to ask how you spotted them,' he said then. 'I'm sure you would tell me if you wanted me to know.'

Magda took her foot off the gas and gave him a wry smile.

'I just wondered if anyone was following you. That's all.'

'And they were.'

She nodded.

'But you had the car? Did you take it when you went to visit the taxi companies?'

'No.' She shook her head. 'They were no good. I got nothing from them. I was soon finished. So I decided to look for you. It was easier by car.'

Jake's turn to nod. He could see that. But there was a lot he couldn't see. The key, for example. Had he left it in the hotel room?

No. He hadn't. He could feel it in his pocket.

But there was a key in the ignition.

'You found a spare key?'

She glanced at him and then at the ignition key, and shook her head. 'It is one Phan made for me. He said it would work with most cars.' She shrugged and added, 'It does with this one.'

'Jesus!' he said, shaking his head, and wondering what she was going to tell him next.

'You are angry?' she asked, shooting him one of her puzzled looks.

'Angry?' He sighed. 'Not angry, no. Just mystified. You saved my bacon back there.'

'Your bacon?'

She was puzzled again. He didn't enlighten her.

'So how many men were there, back there?'

'Four men, in a group, moving fast.'

A team, then. Big enough to cope with most things.

'One had an ear-piece, and was speaking into the sleeve of his jacket. A microphone, I think.'

He nodded. They were well-tooled. And no doubt getting instructions while they were on the move.

'Did you recognize any of them?'

'Maybe the one speaking,' she said slowly, frowning. 'I could have seen him before. I'm not sure.'

'What did they look like?'

'The usual.' She shrugged. 'They were hard men. Perhaps aged in their thirties. Experienced, I would say. And very fit, and strong.'

'I was lucky,' Jake concluded.

'Yes, you were.'

'Thanks to you, Magda.'

She just shrugged. All in a day's work. He really did wonder about her.

They returned to the hotel, brought each other up to date on their enquiries and took stock. Thanks to the car park caretaker, Jake had more to report than Magda. Basically, she had struck out at the other two taxi companies, as he had with the one he visited. Even pleading her case as an abandoned wife searching for her husband had elicited nothing more than unwanted cups of tea.

'Ugh!' she said with a shudder. 'The tea was terrible. Very, very strong – and full of milk.'

He grinned. Magda preferred her tea weak and with a slice of lemon.

'You're just not used to a working man's tea.'

'And I hope I never will be. So. Tell me what you learned.'

'Nothing from the taxi office. On the way back, as you know, I decided to call in at Freddie's old flat again. It's empty now. That woman has gone.'

'You went inside?'

He nodded. 'Even though I didn't have a special key made by Mr Phan, I managed to get inside. But I found nothing new. Then as I was leaving the building, I saw a man sweeping up at the entrance to the underground car park. I had a chat with him. He works there, looking after the car park. I asked him if he knew Freddie. Turned out he did. Great pals, apparently. But, sadly, Freddie had moved out, and he didn't know where he is now.'

'How would he know Freddie?'

'He's a car enthusiast.'

'Who is – the man or Fat Freddie?'

'Fat Freddie.'

'But the woman in the flat said he didn't have a car.'

'She was wrong. Mistaken – or lying. The car park attendant told me a lot about Freddie's car. It's a bit special, apparently.'

He told her the rest of the tale. She listened without interrupting.

'So what are you thinking?' she asked when he'd finished.

'I'm thinking you can hardly drive a car anywhere these days in England without being photographed and subjected to automatic licence plate scrutiny and recognition. I'll ask Bob to see what he can come up with.'

Bob said, 'You've got the reg number?'

'Yeah.'

Jake pushed the piece of paper he'd written it on across the table, avoiding the small pool of beer that had gathered in the centre of the table. Bob studied the slip of paper, seemingly looking for hidden meaning in the string of alpha-numeric characters.

'Beamer, eh? I wonder why we hadn't picked that up?'

Jake didn't know if he meant the car or the number, but he shrugged anyway. He could have suggested Bob simply didn't know the right people to talk to, but he didn't. It might have upset him. He prided himself on being an old-school copper who knew the streets.

'I'll see what I can do,' Bob said, carefully folding the slip of paper and putting it away in his pocket.

'So there's a chance?' Jake asked, knowing the answer but prepared to give Bob the opportunity to demonstrate his professional knowledge and expertise.

'A very good chance. Cameras are everywhere these days. Nigh on every car in the country is probably photographed nearly every day of the year.'

He paused and looked around with interest. 'This your local?'

'Never been here before in my life.'

The Elephant and Duck was just a pub he'd spotted when he'd been looking for the taxi company.

'I thought you'd be able to remember the name without me having to write it down for you,' he added with a grin.

'Cheeky bugger! Still… Silly bloody names a lot of the pubs have these days, don't they?'

'Not like the Red Lion or King's Head, you mean?'

'Aye. You're right.' Bob gave a weary sigh. 'So where are you staying, now you're in London?'

'Nowhere in particular. And nowhere for long.'

'Meaning you don't want to tell me?'

Jake nodded. 'There is that. I'm not telling anyone. It's safer. Fogarty had another go at me yesterday. At least, it was probably him.'

'Here? In London?'

'Yeah. I'm no safer here than I was in Europe. He's got a long reach.'

Jake told him about his narrow escape from the car park, without mentioning either Magda or Kunda. He still wanted her to remain invisible and unknown. Kunda, too, for some reason. Some things he wanted to keep to himself for now. Instinct told him it was safer that way. He would trust no-one. Even the folk on his own side could leak.

'We've got to get him,' Bob said, looking grim. 'Fogarty, I mean. We can't go on like this.'

Jake couldn't agree more. He just didn't know yet how they were going to do it.

Chapter 37

Bob phoned early the next morning.

'He's been spotted,' he said without preamble. 'At least, the car has.'

'Ah! Where and when?'

'Every fucking where! It's been seen hundreds, thousands, of times in the past few months.'

Jake nodded with satisfaction, and with growing excitement.

'I can't tell you where he's living, mind. The sightings have all been on main roads.'

That made sense. Jake thought for a moment and said, 'What sort of data have you got? What form is it in?'

'It's a list of places and times, and a spatial distribution map. Interestingly, the map shows a heavy concentration in north-west London. So that's probably where he'll be living.'

'North-west London?' Jake said with a smile. 'That cuts it down a bit.'

'Yeah, well.'

'Email me what you've got, Bob.'

'It's on its way, bonnie lad!'

Exciting times. Jake took one look at the map that came through on his phone. Then he went out to find a printer. Having a physical map on a sheet of paper would be better, but he also wanted one on a much bigger scale, preferably one with street names.

With a Google search, he found a print shop just a few streets away. So off he went. Happily, they said they could produce what he wanted, once they understood his need.

'It's for a school geography project,' he explained to the man running the machines.

'Yeah? So what are the dots?'

'Places where a road accident has occurred in the past year.'

'I'd have thought there would have been a lot more than that.'

'Oh, these are just the fatalities and serious injuries,' he improvised, hoping the guy didn't question him further.

'It might be worth doing this with pubs?' the machine operator suggested.

'In case there's a correlation? Drink-driving, you mean?'

'No. Just the pubs. In case there's any we don't know about,' he said with a grin.

'Right. Good idea. Then we could tick them off as we visit them.'

'And have two sets of plans. One showing all the pubs, and the other showing the pubs we've visited.'

'And a third one,' Jake said, entering into the spirit of the thing, 'showing those we haven't been to yet.'

'Now you're talking!'

Back at the hotel, Jake unfolded the map and together with Magda, pored over it. Where they had to concentrate was immediately clear.

'The Harrow area,' he said. 'That's where most of the sightings have been.'

'As far from Essex as you can get, and still be in London,' Magda pointed out.

'Makes sense, doesn't it?'

They managed to narrow it down quite a bit more, using a variety of methods, but they were still left with a pretty big area.

'Somewhere in here,' Jake said, using a marker pen to describe a circle on the map, 'is where Fat Freddie is living – hopefully. Let's see if we can find him before Fogarty does.'

They started driving around the streets, ticking them off on the map, one at a time. They were looking for an elderly black BMW, possibly still with the reg plate they knew about. Maybe it would be parked out on the street. Maybe. Forlorn hope, probably, but they had to do something while they waited for a better idea to strike.

After a couple of hours they gave it up.

'This isn't going to work,' Jake said with a reluctant sigh.

Magda agreed.

'You probably thought that all along?' he suggested.

'Yes, I did. We need some other way, some better way of finding the car – or this Freddie.'

'I can't argue with that. Any suggestions?'

'Perhaps we should return to the hotel and talk about it,' she said with a smile. 'Anyway, there are better things we could be doing than this.'

His feelings exactly.

One of the better things to be doing was to climb into bed, reactivate their love life and relax. Since arriving in London they had been on edge, racing around like a tornado, and now the storm had petered out. Exhaustion and disappointment, frustration as well, had come together to stop them in their tracks. It was time to recuperate.

They made love in a gentle, unhurried way. Took their time and rediscovered each other. They had always been good together in bed, and so it was now, too. Magda was especially attentive to his preferences, and Jake managed for a time to put aside all his reservations about her. He still didn't trust her. He wasn't going to forget how she had deceived him, but equally he wasn't going to forget how they had always been with each other.

Thinking about it logically, he knew things had been pretty good between them back in the Algarve, even though their respective histories had been unknown. It hadn't troubled him then. Why should he be so bothered now that he knew so much more about her? Did he really think she was still working for Kunda?

He didn't know. Perhaps it was simply that he did know so much more about her now, and wasn't entirely sure that she really had swapped her allegiance. Kunda had obviously played a big part in her life. Was all that over, as she insisted? He couldn't be sure. But logic said he should just accept the present, as he used to do, and forget about Magda's history.

Logic. He gave a wry smile. That wasn't the answer to everything. Look where he was right now! But what he could do was keep a little bit of himself back, just in case, even though he knew Magda had saved him back at Freddie's old flat. Embrace life, but beware of the unsavoury possibilities it had to offer. That would have to do for now.

'What are you thinking, Jake?'

'What a difference a day makes,' he said with a smile.

'A good difference?'

'Very good,' he said, nuzzling her neck.

'Oh!' she said, rising to the challenge. 'You remember what I like.'

He grinned and did it again. Then one thing led to another, all over again.

Afterwards they lay together quietly for a while; in Jake's case, listening to the faint sound of traffic in the busy street beyond the heavy curtains, and trying not to start whenever a door slammed somewhere as the maids went about their business.

'What shall we do now?' Magda asked sleepily.

He yawned and removed his stiffening arm from beneath her head. 'Phone for room service?' he suggested. 'Order some lunch?'

She giggled. 'Lunch? What time is it?'

'I have no idea, but I'm sure they'll find us something, whatever the time is.'

'You're hungry?'

'A little. Peckish more than hungry. But I wouldn't mind something to eat, and a bottle of beer to go with it.'

'Is there beer in the mini-bar?'

'I think so – unless you've drunk it?'

She giggled again and sat up. 'Order lunch for us, then, while I have a shower.'

'What would you like?'

'Anything,' she said, slipping out of bed.

He ordered a couple of omelettes, and salad and a bowl of wedges to share. It was while he was doing that that he suddenly thought of a sure way of finding Freddie's car.

Chapter 38

He took some finding, Fat Freddie. Hendrik's contact said he'd dropped out of sight, like all the others in Witness Protection. They were just gone.

'We pay you good money,' Hendrik pointed out. 'Find him.'

'It won't be easy.'

'Find him. You've got a week.'

'I don't know if...'

'You've got a week,' Hendrik said, ending the call.

'He'll find him,' Hendrik said. 'They've got resources we don't have.'

'Yeah.' Fogarty sighed and looked morose. 'Not like the old days, is it?'

'Computers, you mean?'

'Computers, online – and all the rest of it. Mobile phones and Facebook. Fucking Twitter! You don't do Twitter, do you?'

Hendrik laughed. 'No, but I would if it was useful.'

'Useful?' Fogarty scowled. 'How much of it – any of it – is useful?'

'Well, like I said, I don't use it myself. But if those we pay good money to can find out what we need to know, why not?'

'You're too modern, Mike.'

Hendrik laughed. 'What do you want to do instead – try to beat it out of somebody?'

'Now you're talking!' Fogarty said, laughing with him. 'So is this guy going to come up with Freddie?'

'He'd better. He won't get much enjoyment out of the rest of his life if he doesn't.'

'Pleased to see you haven't gone soft while I've been away,' Fogarty said, still laughing.

Hendrik's expectations were justified. A few days later, the paid man came back with an address.

'You're telling me he lives there? For sure?'

'Well, he owns it. I haven't been there to check it out, though. I don't do that sort of thing myself.'

No, of course you don't, Hendrik thought. You just sit on your arse and play with your fucking computer!

'How did you find it?' he asked.

'That's a professional secret.'

'How did you find it? I want to know if it's worth me checking it out.'

With a big sigh, the caller said, 'You wouldn't understand if I told you. Basically, the computers found it. I fed them a name, and they scanned for it.'

'Clever.'

'Not really. It's just what we do here.'

Hendrik nodded. 'OK. Thanks.'

'I can't do this sort of thing very often, you know. Somebody might pick up on it. You understand?'

'Yeah. Don't worry about it.'

When he told Fogarty, Fogarty gave a grim smile. 'If he's right, this once will be enough. You should have told him that.'

'We don't want him sleeping easy at night, do we?'

'No. That's true. Cheltenham, eh? Nice place, Cheltenham. I used to like it there in Gold Cup week.'

Fogarty thought about it, frowned and added, 'I always used to wonder what they did in that big place on the edge of town. GCHQ, or whatever they call it.'

'They look for terrorists – and Fat Freddie!'

Fogarty chuckled. 'Useful contact, that guy.'

Hendrik nodded. 'I don't use him very often, but at times like this he's a good investment.'

'Well, let's go and see if he's right.'

Chapter 39

Jake knew he should have thought of it earlier. Freddie had been gone from his flat many, many months, and in that time there was a very good chance that his much cherished BMW had needed a tax renewal. Possibly an MOT, as well.

Freddie would be aware that police cameras could identify un-taxed vehicles electronically these days, and that such vehicles were often traced and stopped. He wouldn't want that to happen to him. Yet he would also want to use the car from time to time. He wouldn't want it just to sit in a garage somewhere for him to look at and polish. That wouldn't do the moving parts any good at all.

To stay legal, Freddie would have had to report a change of address to the DVLA. He would have been on dodgy ground otherwise.

Time to phone Bob again.

It was a fine mock-Tudor house in a tree-lined street, a much superior residence to Freddie's old flat. Well-maintained, too, from the look of it. Not a rental property. So he must have bought it. Used his own money, or a small part of the missing twenty million quid.

Perhaps he'd even had the house all along? Successful career guys in his line of work often prepared well in advance for retirement, or for the day when the wheels came off, which they usually did in the end. Now, with the help of Bob and the DVLA, they had found it at last.

They sat in the car for a few minutes, assessing the situation. Nothing happened.

There were no lights on in the house, and nobody came or left. No sign of the car, either.

'I wonder if the car is in the garage,' Magda said eventually.

'Perhaps. Or he might be out in it somewhere. Anyway, it doesn't look as if anybody is at home at the moment. I'll go and take a look. You stay here.'

'No. I will come.'

'It's raining,' Jake pointed out.

'If you don't want me with you, just say!'

He smiled and shrugged. She was recovering. Back to her old self. As prickly and pushy as ever. Maybe she thought he was going to scoop the money and run – without her.

'Come on, then. Let's go.'

It was a wet night, and the trees and shrubs in front of the house were dripping sheets of icy rainwater. The distant Algarve seemed more alluring than ever. Jake pulled up the collar of his coat. Magda shivered, but he didn't feel sorry for her. She'd had the chance of staying where it was warm and dry, and safe. Now she would just have to put up with it.

Up close, there were still no lights to be seen anywhere in the house. Magda tugged at his sleeve and pointed to a car standing in deep shadow towards the rear of the house. They walked down the short drive to take a closer look.

Jake nodded with satisfaction. They'd found it. This was the car, all right.

'We're in the right place,' he murmured.

Magda nodded.

He led the way to the front door and rang the bell. It was definitely working. He could hear it chiming away in the distance. But no-one answered.

It looked like Freddie really wasn't home. That gave them the chance to get out of the rain and do a bit of poking around. He was curious to know how Freddie was running his new life, and if he was aware of the danger he was in. He hadn't forgotten about the money, either.

Assuming the front door was heavily defended, he looked for an easier way of getting inside. He found it in a small window at the back of the house. He tapped out the glass and reached inside to open the window. Then he climbed in, to find himself in a back scullery where Freddie kept his boots and the washing machine.

He sniffed and grimaced. Then he turned to warn Magda, but she had followed him inside already, which was a bit of a nuisance. He really would have preferred her to be back in the car and safely out of the way, especially now. Sooner, rather than later, she was going to ask about the smell.

Chapter 40

'Remember me, Freddie?' Fogarty asked when the front door opened.

A startled face peered at him for a moment. Then the door slammed shut. Fogarty smiled grimly and turned to study the drizzle-soaked garden.

'Nasty night,' he said in a conversational tone.

Hendrik nodded. 'Just right.'

'It is. Just what we want. Ah! Here we are.'

Smiling again, Fogarty turned back to face the front door as it re-opened.

'We got him,' the man holding the door said, grinning. 'Just like you said, he was leaving by the back way.'

Fogarty nodded. 'Anybody else in the house?'

'Doesn't seem to be.'

'Good. Well, let's get started,' he said with a sigh.

As Fogarty had half-expected, Freddie knew nothing about the missing money. At least, that was what he said. After an hour of questioning, bits of Freddie and blood all over, Fogarty was inclined to believe him. He gave the nod, and one of the two men working Freddie over finished him off with the knife he had been using to such terrible effect.

Fogarty turned to leave. Hendrik followed him.

'So where does that leave us?' Fogarty wondered as they walked back to the car, parked a couple of blocks away.

'Well,' Hendrik said, 'there used to be Penrose in Yorkshire and Gregory in Scotland, but sadly they're no longer with us. The Tenerife boys said neither of them knew anything anyway.'

Fogarty thought for a moment and then shook his head. 'No. Neither of them had the brains they would have needed to grab the money.'

Hendrik used the remote to unlock the car.

Pausing a moment before he got in, Fogarty said, 'And the Czechs will take care of that guy from Portugal now he's on their patch. Who else is there?'

'No-one really. Just Nicci in Crete.'

'It has to be him, doesn't it?'

'It looks that way now, but I'm not so sure we should bother.'

Fogarty got in the car. 'Why not?'

'Well, Crete is a long way away, and outside our comfort zone. Then I'm conscious of the time we're spending on all this. We need to get you somewhere safe, and soon.

'Maybe we should just forget about the money from the heist. It's long gone, after all. Just send the Tenerife lads after Nicci.'

'Well, I hear what you say, Mike, but this is personal. Besides, Crete isn't that far away. I know we can't fly, but the yacht will get us there in a just a few days. I want to carry on, as we planned.'

Hendrik started the engine. 'We still need to start planning to get you away to Cuba, or wherever.'

'Fair enough. I agree. Why don't you get the ball rolling?'

As they pulled away from their parking spot, Fogarty added, 'Funny about Fat Freddie, wasn't it?'

'What was?'

'Well, apart from trying to get out the back door at the beginning, he just gave up. I always thought he had more about him than that.'

'He was scared shitless,' Hendrik said with a chuckle. 'Understandable, really.'

'I misjudged him,' Fogarty said, shaking his head.

'Well, that won't happen again.'

'No, it won't.' Fogarty began to laugh. 'You're right there!'

Chapter 41

Jake didn't open the door into the main part of the house immediately. Instead, he switched on a light and turned to Magda.

'I don't think you should go any further,' he told her. 'What we're going to find will not be very nice. You don't need that experience.'

'I know what that smell is,' she said in an even tone. 'You don't need to worry about me, Jake.'

He was less surprised than he would have been before all this started, but he was still pretty damned surprised. He just looked at her for a moment. Then he shook his head. He could see she meant it.

'Let's get on with it,' she suggested.

With a sigh, he turned to open the door that led into the kitchen.

What was left of Freddie was in the main living room. It wasn't a pretty sight. His death had been far from easy. In fact, his last hour or so didn't bear thinking about.

Blood, and other liquid matter, had spread far and wide across the room. The mountain of bare flesh in the middle of it was where it had all come from. Intent on keeping well clear, Jake stayed in the doorway. Magda, without a sound, stood beside him. They could see what they needed to see without going any closer.

Struggling to stay calm and objective, Jake said, 'We were

too late to help Freddie, sadly, but I think we can be sure of one thing.'

'I agree,' Magda said quietly. 'Freddie did not know where the missing money is.'

Jake's thought exactly. Much of the poor man's suffering would have been unnecessary if he had been able to tell Fogarty what he wanted to know.

'Come on,' he said, turning away. 'We found Freddie, but we're not going to find anything else here. Let's get out.'

He headed for the front door, too uncertain of his stomach to risk clambering back out through the window. Magda followed him.

'You all right?' he asked as he shut the door after them.

'Yes.'

'You're sure?' he insisted, expecting her to collapse into a vomiting heap any moment.

'You don't need to worry about me, Jake.'

'No? You're going to tell me you've seen that sort of thing – or worse – before?'

'Stop it, Jake!' she said sharply. 'You should know by now that I am not an innocent.'

Indeed he should, he thought wearily as they headed back to their car. Indeed he should. Long before now, he had realized that Magda was not your average young woman.

They sat in the car and took stock. Taking stock was something they seemed to need to do a lot of. Either they were hitting their faces against a blank wall or something unsettling had happened. Often it was both.

'Well, we found Freddie,' he said with a sigh.

Magda nodded. 'What is left of him, now the torturers have finished.'

'Yeah.' He thought for a moment before adding, 'Fat Freddie was a career criminal – another one – and probably did a lot of bad things in his life, but...'

'He didn't deserve to die like that,' Magda finished for him.

Jake nodded. Exactly.

'What now, Jake?'

Now? Well, now there was only one person left of the group Bob had asked him to warn about Fogarty's release. And there was still the money, of course. Not forgetting that.

'First, I need to meet Bob and bring him up to date. Then we'll go to Crete.'

'Crete, yes,' Magda said, nodding. 'Somewhere warm and dry will be pleasant.'

Pleasant? Only if we can avert more bloodshed, he thought. And if we can't, let's hope the blood isn't ours.

'But before that, Jake, I think we need to rest for a day or two.'

'What do you suggest?'

'You can see Bob. Then I would like to see a little more of England. Particularly, I would like to see your old home. Is that possible?'

'I suppose so,' he said with surprise. 'Yes, it's possible.'

This woman, he thought wearily. She just continues to astonish me.

Chapter 42

Jake had wondered what it would be like to see his old place again, his isolated cottage in the Northumberland hills. Well, it had been a cottage once, when he lived there. By the time he left, though, it had been a burned-out ruin. For several years he had tried not to think about it. Now? Well, nothing had changed. It was still a burned-out ruin, a charred and blackened heap of stones. The only difference he could see was that now there were healthy clumps of nettles and a few thistles growing amongst the rubble.

At one time, Bob had been going to help him with rebuilding the cottage, but that had never happened. Bob had been too busy, as a serving police inspector, and Jake had lost heart, given the immensity of the job. He hadn't had the money to pay a builder to do the work for him, either. So nothing much had happened at first, and then for several years afterwards nothing at all had happened.

He stopped the car on the track, and turned it round. Then they got out and stood and stared, taking in the dereliction and the sheer loneliness of their surroundings.

After a few moments, Magda said, 'So this is where you lived, Jake?'

'For a while, yes. A couple of years.'

She turned and gazed around at the surrounding moorland, the mix of grass and heather, that stretched for miles. Not a tree in sight. Nor another building. Fern Cottage – what was left of it – was four miles from the nearest village, and from anything else man-built. But in its snug little valley, it had defied the isolation and the elements very well for a long, long time. Many generations of hill shepherds and their families had lived here before it had been abandoned by them and Jake had taken up residence.

They walked up to the sandstone scarp overlooking the cottage. From there, on a clear day, you could see the North Sea, as well as a lot more moorland. A pair of circling crows overhead inspected them, uncertain perhaps if they were foe or food. You had to be opportunistic to live up here. The handful of sheep grazing quietly nearby scarcely noticed their presence. Jake heard a curlew call, and then he glanced up at the skylarks chattering overhead.

Once again, Magda surprised him when she spoke. 'Your enemies attacked from up here?' she asked.

'Enemies?'

'The cottage did not burn down all by itself.'

He gave a grim smile and nodded. 'Yes, that's what happened, all right. A long time ago.'

It was uncanny how Magda could still take him unawares with her questions and observations. Right now, she seemed to be thinking like a soldier on the battlefield, eyeing and evaluating the landscape like a military tactician.

'What a life you must have led, Magda!'

She shrugged but made no comment. They stayed a few more minutes. Then they turned to head back down to the car.

'It is beautiful here,' Magda said, with a last wistful look around at the view.

Jake nodded. He had always thought so. Desolate, lonely, but quietly beautiful. In recent years he had almost forgotten that.

'Could you live here again, Jake?'

He shrugged. 'I don't know. Maybe.'

That had always been his intention. Until Bob had involved him in his quest to bring Fogarty down, rebuilding the

180

cottage had been top of his to-do list. Only lack of resources and insufficient energy had stood in his way.

Now? Now it was quite a while since he had last thought of it.

'Let's go to Crete,' Magda said, sensing his unsettled mood and taking his hand.

Chapter 43

They left that evening, sharing a flight from Newcastle Airport with lots of Geordie holidaymakers. The accents and excited chatter all around them gave Jake something to smile about, and made him feel quite nostalgic.

Magda didn't understand. 'Are they English?' she whispered, puzzled by what she was hearing.

'Certainly they're English,' he assured her. 'Technically, at least.'

'Technically?'

'It's God's own country, here, up in the north.'

'I understand.'

He doubted that.

They landed in Heraklion at a god-awful hour. Jake's watch said it was 2.30 in the morning, but the captain told them all it was a couple of hours later than that. Dawn would soon be breaking.

Magda had managed to doze a little during the flight, but Jake hadn't. His mind was forging ahead to the task of finding Nicci, and hoping they could do it while he was still alive. That would be no mean achievement, considering their success rate so far. Himself and Nicci were now the only ones left on Fogarty's hit list.

He really hoped they would do better with Nicci, not least because he had quite liked the guy. During their ill-fated, short association, Nicci had behaved decently towards him.

Just another career criminal he might be, but Jake was prepared to make all sorts of allowances and excuses for Nicci that he wouldn't have made for the likes of Fat Freddie and the others.

Something that gave him hope was that, in Crete, Nicci was on home ground. This was where he belonged, and where he would be known. As Jake understood it, family and clan still stood for a lot in Crete. They could provide Nicci with the protection he wouldn't have had elsewhere.

Fogarty, on the other hand, was a dangerous, malevolent foreigner. He wouldn't find the odds in his favour here, however much power and influence he could wield in London and leafy Essex.

Jake also believed that when they found Nicci, they would learn what had happened to the missing twenty-million quid. It had to be Nicci who had found a way of spiriting it away. There was no-one else left who could have done it. Fogarty would know that as well, of course. The pressure was building on them all.

That thought brought him back to Magda, sleeping beside him. He still didn't know about Magda. Was she really with him, and on his side, or was she still dancing to Kunda's tune?

He hadn't forgotten the moment of indecision when he interrupted their discussion at the restaurant in Vysoká Lípa. He hadn't been sure then that she would leave with him, and he wasn't sure now that she would stay with him. He might just be serving her purpose, as she was his. A mutual-help pact, he thought with a wry smile. That might be all it was.

There were lots of families with young children on their flight. People looking for sun and sea late in the year, as well as cheap booze and fags. Other stuff, as well, probably. By now, some of the kids were manic after their four-hour incarceration and their sleep deprivation. Let loose in the baggage hall, they took full advantage. The noise was excruciating.

Jake led Magda quickly through it all, heading for the exit, congratulating himself that they carried only hand luggage and didn't have to wait for the carousel to deliver up suitcases.

The day was beginning to dawn when they left the terminal. They took a taxi into the town centre and checked into a hotel for what remained of the night. The new day was going to have to wait until they had caught up on some sleep.

By the time they surfaced, the new day was more than half over. They got up, showered and checked out of the hotel. Then they found a small, quiet café in a side street and ordered a meal that might technically still have been lunch.

'Where does Nicci come from?' Magda asked as they nursed cups of vile coffee. 'You never did say.'

'Not here, or any other town. He grew up on a farm, somewhere in the middle of the island.'

'You think he will have gone back there?'

'Not if he has twenty million pounds, he won't!' Jake smiled and added, 'He told me about the family farm. One of his jobs, when he was young, was to fetch water from the well. They didn't have electricity or indoor plumbing, or much else, either. Plenty to eat, though – in good years.'

'What happened in bad years?'

'I doubt if they ever really went hungry, not here, but...' He broke off with a shrug. 'Who knows?'

Magda pulled a face. 'A primitive life, I think.'

Jake nodded. 'I don't suppose he'll have wanted to take up farming again.'

'So?'

'I still think he might have gone back to the area where he grew up. There was a small town nearby that he talked about once. Town? Not much more than a village, probably. He'll have relatives and friends there. People who know him, and who he trusts. Hell, he might even have rebuilt the town for them!'

'If he has the money,' Magda said with a smile. 'Where is this town?'

'It's somewhere called the Lasithi Plateau. Have you heard of it?'

She shook her head.

'Me neither, apart from the time Nicci mentioned it. We'll hire a car, and make our way there.'

Chapter 44

'The Lasithi Plateau?' Magda said thoughtfully. 'It is what?'

'Well, the name suggests it's a high place, so presumably it's in the mountains.' Jake glanced at her and smiled. 'Other than that, I know nothing.'

They were on their way there, and about to head inland in the Honda CR-V he'd hired in Heraklion. The car was well-worn, both visually and mechanically, but it was like the one he had acquired in the Algarve and left behind in Vysoká Lípa. So the model was familiar, and he knew it to be reliable.

Ah, the Algarve! Would they ever see it again? That wasn't a question for now. Better to concentrate on the moment.

They started to climb. Jake downshifted, and then went down again. Mountains coming up. In fact, he soon realized, the road was cut into the side of a mountain. To their right, there was a sheer drop to the valley, already far below.

He glanced sideways at Magda, who was staring out across the void at the side of the road, and wondered what was going through her head now. Finding Nicci, and perhaps helping to save him? Or something else? Money, perhaps? Or letting Kunda know where they were?

He veered away from where the speculation was taking him, and tried to be positive. Maybe he was misjudging her. There had been times when he would have struggled without her. And that was without even thinking of their life together in the Algarve.

But who was she helping now – him or Kunda? Time would tell.

They were ascending through a series of hairpin bends. Thin coniferous forest swathed the slope above and covered the far side of the valley. One or two very small villages could be seen in the valley that now was far, far below. They passed a parking area where a couple of coaches were standing waiting. A small huddle of buildings cloaked by trees could be seen beyond them.

'It is a monastery,' Magda announced.

'Oh?'

'I saw a sign earlier.'

'So you're keeping your eyes open despite the drop?' he said with a chuckle. 'That's good.'

'Oh, yes,' she assured him. 'Ever since we started our journey my eyes have been wide open.'

What to make of that? It sounded like a gentle rebuke, as if to say she knew he did not trust her.

'Magda, there's something I want to tell you.'

'Yes?'

'However you happened to get into this, and wherever things stand now, I want you to know that I appreciate the support you've given me. I wouldn't have got as far as this without you. I know that. You have no need to fear being undervalued or unappreciated.'

After a moment she smiled and said, 'Thank you, Jake.'

He wondered then if she really was on his side, and had been all along. He would soon find out.

As they climbed ever higher, the woodland on the mountain sides thinned out, revealing bare, rocky ground. There was very little vegetation cover now, and most of that looked dead. Grass and associated plants would be seasonal here, Jake supposed, much like in the Algarve. Trees and shrubs could survive the ferocious heat of summer, even on gravel and bare rock, but there weren't many at this height, and those he could see looked pretty ragged and stunted.

He began to wonder if he had taken the right road. This one seemed like the road to nowhere. It might well take them over the mountains to the far side but it seemed increasingly unlikely that they would find anything like a farm, let alone a village, up here.

The feeling persisted, and grew, as they continued climbing. He began to watch the temperature gauge anxiously. So long in low gears wasn't good for the engine.

Lasithi Plateau? What plateau? Now they were amongst lofty peaks with craggy summits. No sign at all of anything like flat ground. No scope for any sort of farming, either. Even mountain goats would struggle to survive up here. There might be a bit of forestry, but not much. The trees didn't look good for anything but firewood.

They were obviously in the wrong place, he decided. On the wrong road. If he could have stopped safely, he would have, but he couldn't. He kept going, hoping to find somewhere soon where he could pull off the road and turn round. Have a rest, as well. Look at the map, and consider what to do.

Magda sensed his mood, and was thinking along similar lines. 'Maybe this is not where we should be?' she suggested.

He nodded. 'I think you're right. But we'll have to keep going until we find somewhere to stop and turn round.'

Then, suddenly, without warning, they crested a low ridge and, astonishingly, the land ahead of them was flat and stretching out further than they could see. In moments, the land was organized into fields, some with ditches or low stone walls as boundaries between them. Tall crops of maize grew in some, and ripening wheat in others. Trees along the margins were weighed down with apples, their branches touching the ground.

Jake pulled off the road and came to a stop on a patch of baked gravel. He pressed the button that opened his window. Then he sat and stared. The dust their passage had stirred slowly settled around them. Water gurgled along a nearby irrigation ditch. The hot metal of the Honda's engine clicked and creaked, grateful for the chance to rest and recuperate.

'Well!' Jake said at last.

'The Lasithi Plateau,' Magda said quietly, seemingly as awestruck as he was himself.

He nodded. 'This must be it.'

'It is magical.'

That was a good word to use. Magical was how it seemed to Jake, too. They sat there for minutes on end, taking in what they could see, and trying to make sense of a sea of fertile farmland on top of bare and rocky mountains. It made no sense at all. They had entered a hidden world.

A truck passed by, bringing Jake out of his reverie. He re-started the engine and signalled to turn out onto the road. A mile or so along the road he turned off again, and parked outside an information centre.

Then he did what he had been thinking of doing for some time.

Chapter 45

He dumped Magda. He'd been thinking of it for a while. Now he did it.

'Stay here,' he said. 'There's a guesthouse across the road if you want it. Phone for a hire car if you just want to get out of here. Otherwise, I'll pick you up when I come back.'

As he got back in the car, she stared at him with a look he hadn't seen before. It started as bewilderment, and then became pure hatred and contempt.

'You're leaving me here?'

He nodded and slammed the door shut. Then he started the engine and drove away, without once looking in the rear-view mirror.

There were twenty-three villages on the Lasithi Plateau, an area of thirty square miles at an elevation of over 3,000 feet. He had never been before but he had heard about it from Nicci, and now it all came back to mind. This strange, lost world high in the mountains that he was actually seeing for the first time.

As they had just done themselves, Nicci had said you climbed up and up, round the hairpin bends, up above the forest line, and up past the barren, craggy mountain sides where nothing grew until at last you came to the plateau. There, despite the altitude, you came upon a landscape of fields with growing crops – potatoes, wheat and maize, for example – and trees weighed down by their crops of apples.

Traditionally, there were little windmills, too, to draw up the water needed for irrigation. Truly, a lovely, picturesque place.

And there people had lived for millennia, and at times had suffered for centuries.

The Venetians had countered rebellion by massacring everyone they could find, and for 200 years banning people, on pain of death, from setting foot there. The Turks had tried the same approach, although their version hadn't lasted so long. The Germans, too, had exacted a heavy toll of human life during their twentieth century military occupation. In truth, the people were used to it. The plateau had always been a place that nurtured free spirits and fierce thoughts of independence.

So, inevitably, people who chose to live there were used to pain, and perhaps expected it still. As, no doubt, did Nicci, Jake thought. He must be well used to pain and trouble. Always had been. Could he really have believed that here, of all places, he might avoid more of the same?

Jake shook his head. Nicci should be so lucky!

All he had to do now was find him, hopefully still alive and in one piece.

He had dumped Magda for a number of reasons. One was that he still wasn't sure he could trust her now he was so close to the end of the hunt.

A related reason was that he just didn't want to risk her telling Kunda where Nicci was. Better, safer anyway, if she simply didn't know.

Finally, this was the endgame, and for that he had always worked alone.

For all he knew, he wasn't the only person in Crete seeking Nicci. There were certainly two other strong possibilities: Fogarty and Kunda. Whether they were working alone or in tandem didn't matter. That they could be out there somewhere was all that mattered, and he knew they probably would be. Twenty million pounds said so, and so did the lure of revenge.

So he would find Nicci and talk to him, and take it from there. It felt better to be doing that alone. A couple of miles down the road, he stopped the car and consulted a map provided by the hire company. It wasn't much of a map but it had on it the information he needed. The main road on the plateau was a circle that connected all the villages. The village he wanted was on the far side of the loop, perhaps ten miles away. Not far at all.

Something he hadn't told Magda was that this wasn't going to be like looking for Fat Freddie. For one thing, he knew where Nicci was likely to be – if he was here in Crete at all. He knew the name of Nicci's home village. Nicci himself had told him it.

Jake hadn't told Magda. Keeping the knowledge to himself might upset Magda, and might even end his relationship with her, but he was determined there would be no possibility of leaks. Keeping Nicci alive was more important than Magda's feelings. Too many other people had died already. He and Nicci were the last ones left on the at-risk list. He didn't want it to get any shorter.

Tzermiado, the capital of the Lasithi region, was the location he had in mind for Nicci. Capital? It was a village of a thousand people. Still, it counted for a lot at that altitude.

Jake took it all in as he drove along the main street. Quite a few shops and cafés. Even a modern hotel, with lots of tables outside for visitors. He spotted a small café further along the main street that looked promising. Time to park, and walk.

The café seemed to be a family business, with the wife cooking on an open range and the husband serving table. Both were old and slow, seasoned and well used to the ways of the world. Nothing would surprise them, possibly with the exception of waking up again tomorrow.

Two middle-aged men, farmers perhaps, were sitting at a table, drinking glasses of beer when Jake entered the café.

Otherwise, the place was empty. He sat down at a table towards the back of the room, well away from the window. The man waiting on tables shuffled across to hand him a menu. Jake thanked him and began to study it.

The menu listed a lot of dishes, Greek dishes, all of them meals that would be freshly cooked. Not a hamburger or hot dog in sight. The menu had English translation in brackets. Jake smiled. He had been placed.

When the waiter returned, Jake ordered chicken souvlaki and a beer. The man wrote it down laboriously on a small pad with a pencil stub. When he was done, Jake asked him if he knew Nikos Antonakis, who used to live in London but was from this village.

The man said nothing. He paused and stared hard.

Jake shrugged. 'An old friend,' he said. 'I call him Nicci. He calls me Jake.'

'Jake?'

'My name. Jake Ord. Do you know him?'

But the man had turned away and started shuffling back towards his wife, who had her hand held out for the order. Nothing was said between them. The wife took the written order, studied it and began to reach for what she needed. The man took a bottle from a big cooler, took off the cap, collected a glass and began the long journey back to Jake's table.

'Do you know such a man?' Jake asked.

The waiter shook his head. He could have meant no, or he could have meant he didn't understand English. He set the bottle and glass down on the table. Jake smiled his thanks and reached for the bottle. The waiter set off back to the counter, where the tomatoes, onions and whatever else went into the meal were being fried noisily by his wife.

Jake poured some of the beer into the glass and took a sip. Time passed slowly, as it often does in such places. But eventually the woman brought over his meal. It smelled delicious, and he was ready for it. He thanked her.

'Jake Ord?' she said.

'That's me.'

She nodded and turned away. He followed her with his eyes as she hobbled back to her cooking station behind the counter. The man was no longer in sight. It felt as if something was happening.

Chapter 46

A young couple came through the doorway and occupied a table near the window. They began to study the menu. Jake continued eating. Two men sat down at another table near the window. The woman who did the cooking took them a tray containing glasses and bottles of beer. They hadn't even had to ask. It was getting busy. And there was no sign of the old man. Jake concentrated on enjoying the fried chicken pieces in his meal. They were coated with something spicy and crispy.

Then Nicci appeared, seemingly via a back door. Suddenly he was there. It took a moment or two before Jake registered his arrival. He fitted in so very well, with his old, dusty, nondescript clothes and battered leather cap. Just another working man come in from the fields to quench his thirst and find something to eat. It was the beaming smile that gave him away as he approached.

'Jake! It is you,' he said with delight. 'How are you, my friend?'

'Very well, thank you,' Jake said with a grin.

He held out his hand and moved to stand up. Nicci shook his hand but motioned him to stay where he was.

'I couldn't believe it when Andros said you were here. I had to come to see for myself, even though I knew it was probably a trap.'

Jake noticed that the old man, Andros presumably, was back in the café.

'So you've heard, have you?'

'About Fogarty? Yes. I heard.' Nicci shrugged. 'For a long time I expected something. Now we will wait and see. But what are you doing here, Jake?'

'I came to warn you about Fogarty. Inspector Robson – remember him? He asked me to find and warn everyone at risk once Fogarty escaped. Apparently all of you with Witness Protection had dropped out of sight. And I'm in Fogarty's sights, as well,' he added.

Nicci shrugged and looked thoughtful. 'Crete is a long way from London, and Lasithi is even further.'

'Maybe not far enough, though. He's moving fast, Nicci. You and I are the only ones left.'

'What do you mean?'

'Just that. The others on the list have been murdered, and he nearly got me as well a couple of times.'

'Where were you? London?'

Jake shook his head. 'Portugal. The Algarve, actually. I thought I was safe. If Bob Robson hadn't warned me, I don't think I would have survived.'

'Let's have another beer,' Nicci suggested, looking thoughtful.

He turned and gestured to Andros, pointing to the bottle on the table and to them both. Andros nodded.

'An old friend?' Jake asked.

'Cousin. But yes. Andros and his wife are good friends. Here, Jake, I have many friends. It is not like in London for me here. Many, many friends.'

'And relatives?'

'Oh, yes!' Nicci said with a grin. 'All of them are related to me, even if some of them don't know it!'

'Well, you're looking good, Nicci. I have to say that.'

He was, too. In London Nicci had always seemed a chubby little man. Not now, though. Not here. He looked slimmer and hard as teak. His complexion had darkened, too. He fitted right in, Jake decided.

'It is the work, Jake. I work very hard.'

'Oh? Doing what? Not bookkeeping, surely?'

Nicci shook his head. 'Farming, Jake. I am a farmer now. Perhaps I always was at heart. I like it so much.'

'You bought a farm?'

Nicci nodded.

'Well, all I can say is that you look as if it suits you.'

'Thank you, Jake.'

Farming, eh? His own farm, too. So perhaps he really did have the money. He didn't look as if he had spent much of it on himself, though. What about the farm? How much would that have cost? Not twenty-million quid, not here. He should have plenty left – if he did have it.

'What do you produce, Nicci?'

'Everything!' Nicci said, laughing. 'Everything that will grow here, and that I can grow with a profit. Fruit and vegetables, mostly. Almonds and potatoes, apples and lettuce – and so on. A few sheep and chickens, as well.'

'It sounds idyllic. You've used your time better than me, Nicci. I did nothing in Portugal.'

He had wondered how to raise the subject of money. Now he decided to just come straight out with it. Get it over with.

'Something else I'm doing with Inspector Robson, Nicci, is looking for the twenty million in sterling that was never recovered from the heist. He's retired now, and has a deal with the insurance company. And I have a deal with him. If we find it, we get a small percentage of it to split between us.

'I have to tell you, Fogarty is looking for it as well. And he's taking no prisoners along the way, if you know what I mean.'

Nicci grimaced. 'It was to be expected. Twenty million, you say? And what – you think I have it? Is that why you are here?'

'Nicci, there's only me and you left – and I certainly don't have it!'

Chapter 47

Jake pointed out that Nicci now owned a farm, by his own admission. So he had money. Nicci told him it was the old family farm, the one he had spoken of so yearningly in the past. He hadn't had to pay much for it.

'So you don't have the twenty million?'

'Jake, I ask you,' Nicci said, his arms open wide in entreaty, 'do I look like a man with twenty million pounds?'

He pointed through the window at a battered pickup on the other side of the road. 'See that truck? That's mine, my only vehicle. Is that the truck of a man with twenty million pounds?'

Jake grinned. He had to concede the point. The truck looked in worse shape than the one he had left behind in the Algarve.

'Well, Nicci, Fogarty is looking for it. So he doesn't have it. We found what was left of Fat Freddie, and, believe me, if he'd had it, he would have said so long before Fogarty finished working on him. I pity the others if they didn't have it.'

'And it's not you, Jake?'

'Me?' Jake chuckled and shook his head. 'I wouldn't have signed up to help look for it if I had it, would I?'

'Then maybe it doesn't exist. Maybe there is no missing twenty million.'

'Maybe. But in that case, why does Fogarty believe there is?'

Neither of them had an answer to that question, not one

that settled the matter. But they spent quite a while going all over it again, and again.

'Then there's the Czechs,' Jake added, introducing a whole new dimension to the discussion. 'This guy Kunda.'

'What do you know about him?' Nicci asked suspiciously.

'Not much. But I've met him.'

'How did that happen?'

'It's a long story. Suffice to say, he's looking for the missing money, as well. He's also looking for you and me.'

Nicci swore under his breath. That revelation seemed to worry him more than anything else he'd heard so far.

'But you've seen no sign of trouble?' Jake asked.

'Nothing, nobody.'

Jake nodded. He must have got here first for once. Otherwise Nicci wouldn't still be alive.

Not that it made much difference. A waste of time, really. Nicci had already known about Fogarty, and he didn't have the money. Forget it, he thought despondently. All of it. He'd have been better off trying to find a way to take the battle to Fogarty.

A little later Jake realized it was growing dark, darker than it should have been at that time of day in September. He stopped what he was saying and looked around uneasily.

'There's a storm coming,' Nicci said. 'Let's go to the flat.'

'What flat?'

'I keep a little place in the village. Just a couple of rooms for when I'm too tired, or too drunk, to go back to the farm.'

Jake nodded. The light was strange now, a sort of yellow initially that was moving towards sepia. It was eerie.

'It's nothing,' Nicci said with a shrug.

It seemed to be more than that. Looking around, Jake noticed that the other people in the café were not treating it as nothing. The two men who had been drinking beer got up and left. They jumped into a truck across the street and roared away. A young couple stood up from their table beneath the outside awning and stood looking anxiously along the street. The woman behind the counter, the wife of Nicci's cousin, kept glancing at the window with a frown. Her husband, Andros, Nicci's cousin, busy clearing tables, paused once or twice to look at the window or the doorway himself. He seemed perplexed.

Thunder rolled, and from nowhere a gusty wind arrived to chase rubbish along the street. Cardboard boxes and empty drinks cartons tumbled along the road and were whisked high into the air. People in the street ducked their heads and rushed for cover. The light grew poorer. It became quite dim inside the café. Then the overhead light went out and after a few seconds, flickered back on again with much reduced power.

A pickup truck swept along the street at speed, as if racing to keep ahead of the coming storm. The young couple left the shelter of the awning and trotted away, the woman clutching the man's arm. The overhead light in the café went out again, and didn't come back on this time.

'Maybe we should go?' Jake suggested, feeling restless and unaccountably troubled.

Nicci shook his head. 'Too late. The storm's nearly here. We're all right, though,' he added. 'Nothing's going to happen here.'

Jake wasn't so sure about that. It was a rational response but his unease was still growing by the minute.

'Come on, Nicci. Let's go!'

He stood up and dropped some notes on the table to pay for his lunch and their beer.

'That's too much,' Nicci said, reaching out to push some of the money back at him.

'What does it matter? Leave it!' Jake snapped, grabbing his arm.

Reluctantly, Nicci allowed himself to be pulled to his feet. Jake pushed him towards the door. The woman behind the counter called something, a thank you probably, or perhaps a goodbye. Jake acknowledged her with a wave and steered Nicci out onto the street, where a violent wind blew dust into their faces and made them squint and duck their heads.

'Which way?'

Nicci pointed and started trudging along the street, heading into the wind. Jake glanced behind them and then set off to follow. None of this was good. He didn't like any bit of it. The weather was only one thing. They also needed to be somewhere safe, not out in the open like this. There was no-one else on the street now. No vehicles, either. But he kept his head up as he went after Nicci.

Forked lightning shot across the road ahead, followed by a cannonade of thunder that stopped him in his tracks. He looked around. The street was empty still. Lights to either side, but empty. A fusillade of rain, driven hard by the wind, suddenly hit him in the face. He ducked his head automatically, a reflex gesture, but brought it up again immediately to peer ahead. Vertical sheets of rain were now racing towards them, one after another, mixed with clouds of topsoil from the fields beyond the village and branches ripped from the trees that lined the road.

Squinting into the gloom ahead, he suddenly saw two figures in the centre of the road, walking towards them. He reached out, grabbed Nicci's arm, spun him round and dragged him to the side of the street and into the garden in front of a big, old house.

Nicci found his voice and began to protest.

'Shut up!' Jake snapped, wrapping his hand over Nicci's mouth.

Chapter 48

In the eerie gloom and shrieking wind, Jake kept Nicci still
and quiet until the two figures had passed by. Then he got off
his knees and pulled Nicci up after him. By then, Nicci had
realized something was happening, and he made no protest
as Jake hustled him through the shrubbery in the garden
and out the other side.

'Can we reach your flat without going back into the main
street?' Jake rasped, his voice hoarse with the dust in the air.

Nicci nodded and led the way through a couple more
gardens, and out into a back lane. Struggling against the
wind, they kept going until they reached a hairdressing
salon. To the side of it, a wrought-iron gate gave access to a
flight of stone steps. Nicci opened the gate.

That was when the wind faded and they were suddenly
bathed in light again. The storm was nearly over, Jake
realized, and they were returning to normal daytime. He
paused and glanced around with relief and astonishment.
There was even a hint of sunshine leaking through the
rapidly thinning cloud cover. He glanced up at the window
at the top of the steps as Nicci began to climb.

'Wait!' he hissed.

Nicci spun round. 'What's wrong?'

'Somebody's in the flat. I just saw the curtain move.'

Nicci paused a moment and then shrugged. 'It'll just be my
cousin's girl, Elana. She does a bit of cleaning for me.'

That didn't satisfy Jake but Nicci wasn't going to wait any

longer. He started off up the steps, using the iron handrail for leverage. Uncertain, Jake followed him reluctantly. Nicci might be right, he knew. It was his place, after all.

Nicci fished out his keys and started to fit one in the door lock. Jake stood to one side, tense as a spring. If something was going to go wrong, now would be a good time.

The door swung open. Nicci was surprised and lost his balance, stumbling back against the balustrade.

'Get inside!'

A man stepped forward, gun in one hand, reaching for Nicci.

Jake exploded. He grabbed the hand holding the gun with both of his own hands and swivelled his hip against the man in the doorway.

Surprise was on his side. Three things happened. The gun came free in Jake's clutch. The man lurched forward and cannoned into the balustrade. And Jake followed up by dipping his body and bringing his shoulder up sharply to smash into the man.

Off balance, the man yelped, toppled backwards over the balustrade and disappeared. A dull thud told he'd arrived on the concrete patio below.

A second man appeared in the doorway. Jake levelled the gun at him. The man slammed the door shut.

Jake turned, grabbed Nicci and hustled him down the steps and out into the lane. A passing glance told him the guy who had fallen wouldn't be getting up again. A broken neck meant his head had virtually separated from the rest of him.

'My car's close!' Jake urged as they raced along the lane. 'Just around the corner.'

Nicci said nothing. He just ran, ran faster than Jake would have guessed was possible for him. They reached the car and threw themselves inside. Jake started the engine and they took off fast. The hail of bullets he half-expected didn't come as they sped along the main street, navigating a way through the wreckage and rubbish left by the storm.

'Where to?' Jake asked once they had left the village behind.

'The farm,' Nicci said in a dull tone. 'Keep going along here.'

During the short journey, Nicci began to recover and find some of his old ebullience. 'We'll be OK at the farm,' he said confidently.

Jake wasn't so sure about that. If Fogarty could find them in Tzermiado, he sure as hell could find them on some damned farm. It would just be a matter of time. Time, though, was what they needed. They had to get themselves sorted out.

'Have you got any weapons at the farm, Nicci?'

'Just a shotgun.'

At least it was something, Jake thought with a grimace.

'And I've got this pistol I just took off the guy back at your flat.'

'You did well, Jake. Thanks.'

'We got lucky. And I was expecting something.'

'Well, they certainly took me by surprise,' Nicci said ruefully. A few minutes later he added, 'Here. Take this turning.'

'This it?'

'Yeah. Home sweet home.'

Jake turned off the road and onto a gravelled track that ran towards a timber house a few hundred yards away across small flat fields.

As they trundled over the farmland, Jake looked in vain for some redeeming feature in the landscape. Anything that might contribute to the house's defences. There was nothing. Not a hill or a big rock, a river or a patch of woodland. Nothing. Nothing but a bunch of miserable little olive trees that weren't much taller than the wheat he could see growing in a couple of the fields.

'You on your own here, Nicci? Or do you have someone living with you?'

'Just me. A couple of guys help me out in the fields but they don't live here.'

Jake nodded. Better in one way, but not so good in another. Nobody else to worry about, but nobody to give them a hand, either. They were on their own.

'We'd better call the police,' he said.

Nicci shook his head. 'None here, and the ones that would come from Heraklion wouldn't be much more than traffic cops anyway.'

That was probably right, Jake thought with a grimace. Same as the Algarve. These quiet, rural places were not equipped to deal with the likes of Fogarty. That being the case, he couldn't see how they could stay here for longer than it took to catch their breath.

'So we're on our own,' he said flatly.

Nicci nodded agreement.

Chapter 49

They were wrong about that. They were not alone. Both men stopped, astonished, and stared at the figure sitting at the kitchen table.

'Surprised to see me, Jake?'

'How the hell did you get here?' he asked, shaking his head.

Magda smiled sweetly and said, 'Hello, Nicci. How are you?'

Nicci glowered at her and then stormed around the room, letting fly with what sounded like a long string of Cretan curses.

It culminated with him rounding on Jake and demanding, 'What's she doing here?'

Jake shrugged. 'Beats me.'

He was beginning to recover. His brain was picking up speed again. It didn't matter how Magda had got here. She was here. That was all that mattered. Now they had more important things to think about.

'Get your shotgun, Nicci. I'm going to see if we can hold out here.'

'What about her?'

'Save it, Nicci. She's no threat. We're all going to be dead if we can't figure out a way of holding Fogarty off when he comes.'

'He might not come,' Nicci said sullenly.

'You know better than that, Nicci. Come on! Snap out of it.

And you,' he added, pointing a finger at Magda, 'stay exactly where you are.'

'Yes, sir,' she said sweetly, annoying him even more.

He began his inspection. The kitchen was a fair size. A big family could have cooked and eaten in here, he thought, which was probably what used to happen. Small windows. That was good for reducing the ways a bullet could come in.

Maybe it wouldn't make much difference, though, he decided on second thoughts. It would be a poor, under-strength bullet that couldn't rip through the timber walls of this old house.

The parlour, or whatever Cretans called their posh room, was equally big, and had big windows on two sides. He frowned at that. Crossfire? On the other hand, it meant good visibility. The heavy, wooden furniture – a dresser and various cupboards – were promising. They looked as if they would give better protection from bullets than the walls of the house.

A vividly coloured painting occupied the prestigious centre spot on one long wall. Jake looked at it for a moment. It looked like a human figure that had been broken into a thousand pieces, triangles and squares, each one a different colour. The figure had several eyes. Modern art. He shook his head, and wondered what it did for Nicci. Couldn't be much. A bit less wall to paint, perhaps, when he got round to doing some decorating.

The upstairs rooms all had windows, which meant that if you had enough manpower, you could keep good watch all around the house. The trouble was that they didn't have that kind of manpower.

He paused to take stock. Not good, he decided. The house would give very little protection. For an incoming crew armed with machine guns, it would be like shooting the proverbial rats in a barrel. In fact, the barrel would soon fall to bits if hit by serious bullets. They'd better get out.

'Nicci, we can't stay here.'

'What do you mean we can't stay here? This is my home!'

'It's indefensible, Nicci. When Fogarty's people come, we won't be able to keep them out. Not with one shotgun and a handgun. It can't be done. They'll just shoot the place to bits. We need to leave.'

'Where would we go?'

'I dunno,' Jake said with exasperation. 'Any bloody cave would do!'

He calmed down.

'What about your family? Don't any of them have safer places than this? Even if they don't, the extra manpower would be a help.'

'I'll phone my cousin. We can go there. She'll help.'

'Where does she live?'

'Halkidiki.'

Nicci disappeared into the parlour. Jake followed, to see Nicci dragging a chair over to the wall where the painting hung.

'What are you doing?'

'The painting. I want to take it.'

'Nicci, it's a fucking picture. It's our lives at stake here!'

The logic seemed to make no difference. Nicci climbed up onto the chair.

'It's too late, anyway!' Magda called. 'They're here.'

Chapter 50

'This it?' Fogarty demanded.

Hendrik studied the map on his phone and said, 'It seems to be. Chateau Nicci.'

Fogarty got out of the truck and turned to study the distant farmhouse. It didn't look much. He'd seen better sheds on allotments.

'Home sweet home, eh? Well, Nicci, old boy, you've got a big shock coming. You have to wonder what he's done with the money,' Fogarty said with a chuckle. 'If this is what he's bought, property prices around here must be worse than in London.'

'It's a dump, isn't it?' Hendrik said.

'Well, let's make contact. See what Nicci has to say for himself. Send a couple of men around the back first, to stop him doing a runner.'

While Hendrik was seeing to that, a shot was fired from the farmhouse, making everyone fall flat.

'A suggestion, Ed,' Hendrik said, returning to stand beside Fogarty. 'There's more than one man in there. Probably that guy who knocked our lad off the balcony is with him. Maybe more. And they've got weapons.'

'Well, one we know about. Only a shotgun.'

'Let's see if we can talk Nicci out. No point risking losing anyone else.'

'Talk him out? How the hell are we going to do that? He knows what we've come for. He knows what we're going to do.'

'Even so...'

'OK. You're right. What do you suggest we do?'

'Send a guy with a white flag to tell him we want to negotiate.'

'Negotiate?' Fogarty said with a chuckle. 'Yeah, right. Let's try that first. Then we'll do it the old way. We'll blast them out!'

Chapter 51

Several men spilled out of the truck. Even from a distance, Jake could identify Fogarty amongst them. That was a surprise. Hands-on, eh? In for the kill. Well, they would have to see about that. If nothing else, he was determined to go down fighting.

Fogarty could be seen giving his men instructions, spreading them out around the house. Jake grimaced. They were outnumbered, and probably massively out-armed as well. He didn't know what the hell to do. Meanwhile, bloody Nicci was struggling to get that damned picture off the wall!

He opened a window and fired a round from the shotgun. It did no harm, apart from wasting precious ammunition, and he wanted to let Fogarty know they would defend themselves. It wasn't going to be a walk-over, like with Freddie and the others.

More like Rorke's Drift, he thought grimly. Or Custer's Last Stand. The Zulus, or the Apaches, are coming, and we're heavily outnumbered and running out of ammo!

It didn't seem very funny at all.

He watched intently as Fogarty arrayed his forces.

'Two men at the back of the house,' Magda called from her position on the other side of the room.

And three or four around the truck. Virtually an army. Soon they would move in, he thought grimly. There was no way of stopping them.

Surprisingly, a man approached the house. He strode along the track, waving a stick with a piece of white material hanging from it.

Jake frowned. What was this? A truce offering? They couldn't be surrendering. He wiped the sweat from his face and called out to Nicci. 'See what he wants. I'll cover you. And leave that bloody painting alone!'

With understandable reluctance, Nicci went outside to hear what the messenger had to say. It was simple.

'Fogarty wants his money, Nicci. Agree to give him it, and we can all go home. No trouble. Nobody hurt. End of story.'

'End of me, you mean!'

The man stared at him blankly. 'Whatever. He's giving you fifteen minutes to think about it. Then we're coming in.'

'You might be coming in, but you won't all be leaving – not alive!'

The messenger shrugged and turned to walk away.

Fifteen minutes? Jake mulled it over, trying not to let the tension get to him. Something wasn't right here. Fogarty feeling magnanimous?

Time to talk.

'Nicci, they seem pretty confident you have the money.'

'Dumb fucks! What do they know?'

'Fogarty has reached the end of the road. Somebody has it, and you're the only one left.'

'And you,' Nicci pointed out.

'I don't have it.'

'And I don't, either.'

'Fogarty thinks different.'

'Let him.'

Jake shook his head. He felt exasperated. Worried as well, if he allowed himself to think about what was likely to happen next. But exasperated mostly. He didn't understand the situation. What the hell was Fogarty up to?

'He's lying, Jake,' Magda said softly. 'Nicci's got the money. Some of it, at least.'

'Shut your fucking mouth, bitch!'

Jake swung round and looked from one to the other of them. Nicci raging mad. Magda ice-cool. What the hell?

'Why do you think Nicci wants that painting so much?' Magda asked.

Jake shook his head. 'No idea. You tell me.'

'Because it's worth upwards of five million, in sterling. Maybe close to ten.'

He stared at her, ignoring the muffled rage from Nicci.

'How do you work that out?' he asked in a level tone. 'What do you know, Magda?'

Calm and unblinking, she stared back at him.

'Nicci is a money man. He knows about value, and about profit. Picassos go up in value faster than gold if the market is right.'

'A Picasso? Are you telling me...?'

'I used to do the same thing for Kunda. I converted cash to investments like art.'

'It's just a painting,' Nicci snapped. 'Don't listen to her, Jake. It's a fucking painting, for chrissake!'

'It's a Picasso,' Magda insisted quietly but confidently. 'One in his Cubist style. "The Head of a Woman" is its title. Nicci bought it at auction in New York three months ago. I've just checked on my phone.'

Five minutes of the fifteen gone. Ten to go. Who to believe? A crafty, career money man for a criminal empire, or the woman he loved, who had deceived and betrayed him all the way?

'I want the truth, Nicci. Or I'm turning you over to Fogarty. What's going on?'

Nicci's options were few, and whatever else he was, Nicci was a smart guy.

'OK, OK! I'll tell you how it was.'

'And how it is now,' Jake said.

'Yeah, yeah!'

'Better make it quick, Nicci. We're running out of time here.'

'OK, OK! The quick version is that me and Hendrik managed to get hold of the money everyone is looking for. I won't go into how we did it now, but we did.'

'The twenty million?'

'Yeah.'

'You and Hendrik?'

Nicci nodded and looked uncomfortable. 'We split it,' he said. 'Fifty-fifty.'

Jake took a turn around the room, to stretch his limbs, his mind reeling. He glanced at Magda. She nodded, urging him to go on.

'And presumably Fogarty doesn't know about this?'

Nicci shook his head. 'Fogarty was going away for a very long time. Forever, maybe. Me and Hendrik took the chance.'

'Squeaky-clean Hendrik, the white collar man?'

'Somebody had to stay clean, and Hendrik has always been the man for that. Fogarty trusts him.' He shrugged. 'Hendrik has always done a good job.'

'Until now.'

Nicci said nothing.

'So Hendrik's problem now is that Fogarty got out?'

'Yeah.'

'That's a real big problem he's got,' Jake said, his brain working overtime, looking for a way of using this astonishing information.

Nicci and Hendrik, eh? Who would have thought it? And what would Fogarty think, and do, if he knew? Good question!

'What did you do with your share of the money, Nicci?'

'Bought back the farm my family had lost in one of the depressions that had made them bankrupt.'

'And?'

Nicci shrugged.

'Bought a Picasso?'

'Yeah.'

'No cash left?'

'Not much, no.'

Jake did some quick thinking. All this was very interesting but he couldn't see how he could use it to get them out of here.

Tell Fogarty? What then? Well, after stripping Hendrik of what he had, Fogarty would come in here to take Nicci's share as well. If that happened, there wouldn't be much left of any of them. Except Fogarty.

'A private word in your ear, Jake?' Magda said.

He glanced at her.

'Something you should know. It may help to get us out of here.'

Chapter 52

Magda told him what she had in mind. He listened with increasing incredulity. Still in contact with him? Things were far worse than he had imagined. He wondered what had ever possessed him to trust this woman.

'It is simple,' she said with a shrug. 'I owe him, and he owes me.'

Simple? Not to him, it wasn't. But beggars couldn't be choosers, Jake soon concluded. And there might be a way of using the situation to their advantage. One thing was certain: they couldn't just shoot their way out of here. If they were to get out at all, they had to use whatever assets and knowledge they had.

Magda was the key. Everything would rest on her shoulders, if anything was to happen. She was in a unique position and it made sense to use her.

Jake talked to her fast, sketching the outline of an idea, scarcely a plan, eager to see if she could and would fill in any detail. Wanting to know if, in her opinion, it could be done. Was it possible? It seemed absurd. But what else did they have?

'Is it possible?' he asked.

She nodded. 'Maybe.'

'Will he do it?' Jake asked a little desperately, aware that the fifteen minutes would soon be up.

'He will – for me.'

'Then tell him. And promise him!'

As Magda got on her phone, Jake went to speak to Nicci again.

'It might be possible for us to get out of here, Nicci. But you're going to lose the painting.'

'No way!'

'It's comes down to a straight choice, Nicci. Either you lose the Picasso and your life, or you just lose the Picasso.'

'And what then?' Nicci asked with a cynical laugh. 'Lose the farm, as well?'

'No. You'll be able to stay here, if things go well. You'll be able to keep the farm.'

Jake didn't really need to try to persuade Nicci of anything, because it was going to happen anyway, or not, regardless of what Nicci wanted. But, for the moment at least, it was sensible to keep him on side. They needed him. Nicci had a part to play, too.

'He will do it!' Magda called softly, switching off her phone.

Jake nodded. Then he told Nicci what they wanted him to do. Nicci was extremely reluctant but Jake pushed him through the doorway with a make-shift white flag in hand.

'All you have to do,' Jake had told him, 'is ask.'

'What if Hendrik won't come?'

'It doesn't really matter whether he comes or not, Nicci. Play for time. That's the important thing.'

'Then what?'

'Wait and see, Nicci. The rest of it's nothing to do with you. Just remember, you'll get the farm, and a get-out-of-jail-free card.'

'If I live.'

'There is that,' Jake conceded. 'But we're all in that position, aren't we?'

At first nothing happened.

Watching Nicci through a window, Jake said over his shoulder, 'How long does he need?'

'Not long. Just a few minutes, I think.'

'Let's hope we get them.'

'I hope so, too,' Magda assured him.

Then it started.

The original messenger came forward again to see what Nicci wanted. Nicci told him. The messenger retreated.

After a minute or two of consultation amongst the distant ranks, a different figure came forward.

'Hendrik,' Magda said.

Jake nodded. 'You know him, don't you?'

'I do.'

Jake was reassured. He was also tense and anxious. But at least their ball was in play now.

It wasn't always clear what was happening after that. Jake just hoped the various actors were all reading from the same script.

So far as he could see, Hendrik began exchanging words with Nicci as he walked along the track towards him. Nicci stayed where he was, no more than twenty yards from his own front door, exactly as Jake had told him.

Then a big truck turned off the road onto the track leading to the farm. As it sped along the track, consternation was visibly sparked amongst the group standing around Fogarty's vehicle. Figures spun round. There was some shouting. Hendrik turned to see what the commotion was all about.

The new arrivals wasted no time and took no chances. The truck slewed to a high-speed stop. Then what sounded like a heavy machine gun spoke, and the little group around Fogarty's vehicle all went down in a heap, Fogarty with them.

Wisely, Hendrik stood still and put up his hands. Nicci, on the other hand, turned and dashed for the safety of his own front door, again just as he had been instructed.

The truck started up again and came on down the track. Two men hopped off, took hold of Hendrik and pushed him inside the big double cab. After a brief stop to collect the bodies around Fogarty's vehicle, the truck sped away. It was replaced by a big SUV, a Toyota.

'What now?' asked a breathless Nicci.

Jake shrugged. 'Relax, Nicci. It's nearly over.'

Nicci started to protest when he saw Magda heading for the door with the Picasso.

'Leave it, Nicci,' Jake advised. 'She knows what she's doing.'

Nicci gritted his teeth and shut up.

They watched as Magda walked steadily along the track towards a man standing beside the newly-arrived vehicle. Jake thought he recognized the man as Pavel Kunda. The two met and spoke. Magda showed him the painting. He took hold of it. There was some discussion. Then Magda walked back towards the house, minus the Picasso.

Jake went outside to meet her. 'Is it all right?'

She nodded. 'I believe so.'

'What next?'

She gave a little shrug. 'It is clear. I will go now with Pavel and the Picasso. It will be my job to sell the painting, as I'm the one who knows about such things. Then I will be free to leave. '

'And?'

'We will see.'

'Come back, Magda.'

'Are you sure – after all this? Is it what you want?'

He nodded. 'But only if your debts, and his, are cancelled.'

'They will be.'

'Then if you don't return,' Jake said with a wry smile, 'I'll come looking for you.'

Unsmiling herself, she stepped forward to kiss him on the cheek. Then she turned and walked back towards the waiting Kunda.

Chapter 53

'So,' Bob said, 'as of now, we've got nothing?'

Jake nodded agreement.

'All that, and we've got nowt to show for it!'

'I wouldn't say that, Bob. We're both alive, and we've got our health. Fogarty isn't, and hasn't.'

'There is that.' Bob nodded thoughtfully and looked around. 'You know, I've always liked this pub.'

'Me, too.'

'The Crown Posada. I don't know why I don't come here more often. Did I ever tell you—'

'You did, Bob. Yes. About how some sea captain bought it for his mistress in the long ago.'

They both listened for a few moments to Billie Holliday singing scratchily about her man, on a record player with a stylus.

'It's a wonder they haven't worn that old record out,' Bob said, 'all these years they've been playing it.'

'Still sounds good, though,' Jake pointed out.

'Still sounds good,' Bob agreed.

'Tell me again how it's supposed to work,' Bob said with a weary sigh.

Jake hesitated for a moment, wanting to make sure he repeated what he had said the first time. He didn't want any slip-ups at this stage.

'Just focus on the Picasso, Bob. That's all that counts now.

The remaining money has gone, God knows where. Hendrik had half of it. Kunda abducted Hendrik, and by now he'll probably have Hendrik's share, and Hendrik will be feeding the sharks.

'But we managed to rescue a painting that had been bought with Nicci's share of the money.'

'The Picasso.'

'The Picasso, yes. Which Magda is going to sell. The deal is that half of what she gets goes to Kunda, and the other half comes back to us to give to the insurance company. So we'll be returning to the insurers something like five million quid. Hopefully, we'll get ten per cent of that – half a mill, say – which you and I will split fifty-fifty. You OK with that, Bob?'

Bob grimaced. 'It sounds complicated.'

'Not really.'

Bob thought long and hard before adding, 'And I'm supposed to sell this to the insurance company? They're down twenty mill, and we're offering them five?'

Jake shrugged. 'That's five more than they have right now. They should be grateful to you. All this time after the heist they've got nothing, remember? You were a long shot for them, and you came up trumps. Anything you could recover, no questions asked, you'd get ten per cent. That was the deal, wasn't it?'

'Yeah. But what if they want the whole lot? What we give them and what Kunda has, as well? And what if they want to bring the authorities in on it?'

'That's OK. Tell them to look for it, like we had to do. Tell them we've done all we can.'

'And if they want to know where the five mill came from?'

'Tell them.'

'And about the auction, as well?'

'Yeah. Why not?'

'What about—'

'Look, Bob, tell them whatever the hell you like. I don't care. It'll just be hearsay anyway. You weren't directly involved, were you?'

'That's true,' Bob said with what sounded like relief. Then he added, 'This Kunda feller? He's doing pretty well out of it, isn't he? Maybe fifteen million – and for what?'

'Who? Kunda, did you say?'

Bob looked thoughtful. 'Is that not his real name?'

'Who knows?' Jake said, grinning. 'I don't.'

He shrugged and added, 'What you have to remember, Bob – I certainly do! – is that whatever his name is he saved our lives. The three of us – me, Nicci and Magda – would all have been dead in the next few minutes if Magda hadn't got Kunda to intervene. And Fogarty would still have been alive, and at large.'

'There is that, I suppose,' Bob said with a reluctant grin.

'So far as I'm concerned, Bob, that's all there bloody well is! You can forget the rest of it. Nothing else matters. I'm alive. Nicci is alive. And so is Magda.'

'The mysterious Russian woman?'

Jake nodded.

'The woman who is going to sell this painting for Kunda, and then come back with about five mill for us to return to the insurance company?'

'That's right.'

Bob chuckled and shook his head. 'The optimism of youth! I'm glad you survived, son – don't get me wrong. But, seriously, do you really expect to see her again? Or the money, either?'

Jake just shrugged.

'I thought so!' Bob laughed, patted him on the back and went to get another round in.

It's a bit chilly and damp now. Winter is the cool, rainy season in the Algarve. Jake is thinking of lighting the wood-burning stove. The house will gradually get damp and cold if he doesn't. Tomorrow he will take the old truck to a farm he knows, where he can buy a load of eucalyptus wood and olive logs. It is time to start looking ahead. No good waiting longer. The past is done with now.

He hears a car slow down and come to a stop on the road outside. From where he sits on the veranda, he can't see who it is. One of the neighbours, presumably. Coming home from a shopping trip. Sometimes they turn outside his house, where the road is a little wider.

A car door slams shut. He hears a flutter of voices. A man calls his thanks. The car drives away with a throaty roar.

The gate gives a little squeal as someone opens it, and then squeals again as it is closed. He watches, and waits, thinking about how the hinges on the gate need greasing.

When she comes into view, he lets out the breath he has been holding and gets to his feet. As she walks steadily towards him, he can see the smile grow on her face.

'I am here!'

He holds out his arms and she runs the last few paces.

It went well, she told him later. Perhaps it took a little longer than she had hoped, but so what? In the end, the sale went through fine.

'In New York?'

'In New York,' she confirmed. 'The same auction house where Nicci bought it. They were pleased to see it again. This time it sold for just over fifteen million, in sterling.'

'More than you hoped?'

She shrugged. 'A little, perhaps, but not too much. Nicci had got it cheap.'

'So what happens now to the money?'

'It goes into a joint account we established. Kunda can withdraw no more than half the balance, and the same is true for me. Now we must find out where to send our share, the money for the insurance company.'

Jake thought it through. One thing still bothered him.

'We're free of Fogarty now, but what's to stop Kunda coming after you for the rest of the money?'

'It is simple. First, he and I are in agreement. Our association is at an end. Second, I know too much about him and his business life. I have deposited copies of a detailed statement about them with lawyers in different countries. If anything happens to me, they will be opened and Kunda will be destroyed.'

He had to admit it, he was impressed. All over again! She had thought of everything. She had handled everything that had come her way. Never faltered. It was a lot to live with, for them both. Could they do it?

He rather thought they could. After all, despite everything, she had come back to him, just as she had said she would. What more could he ever have asked or hoped for?

He got up and disappeared into the house for a minute. When he returned, he was carrying an opened bottle of wine and two glasses.

'I know it's a bit on the cool side,' he conceded, 'but let's do it anyway.'

'Yes,' she agreed. 'It was what we were doing that evening all those months ago when you got the first phone call.'

He poured the wine.

'So what next?' he asked after they had toasted each other.

'Here is good for now, I think, Jake. Then in the spring, when we have our share of the money and we are recovered, we should go again to Northumberland and rebuild your cottage. What do you think?'

'I like the sound of that!' He laughed. 'You've thought of everything, haven't you?'

As enigmatic as ever, she said neither yes nor no. She just smiled.